D0402803

edges

léna roy

Farrar Straus Giroux | New York

4619 7611 6/11

www.fsgteen.com

Library of Congress Cataloging-in-Publication Data
Roy, Léna.
   Edges / Léna Roy. — 1st ed.
      p.   cm.
   Summary: New Yorkers Luke, sixteen, and Ava, nineteen, both wind
up in Moab, Utah, trying to put their lives back together after suffering
from the death of loved ones, alcoholism, and other traumas.
   ISBN: 978-0-374-35052-9
   [1. Alcoholism—Fiction.   2. Grief—Fiction.   3. Emotional
problems—Fiction.   4. Family problems—Fiction.   5. Moab
(Utah)—Fiction.]   I. Title.

PZ7.R8128Ed 2010
[Fic]—dc22

                                                        2010008417

For Rob

friday

one

Luke nearly banged his head on the door frame as he moved the last of his meager possessions into the trailer. He remembered to duck just in time, cursing his height. This last item, his mother's painting, was the most cumbersome thing he had brought from New York. He leaned it against the wall and looked around. It was a relief that the trailer was already modestly furnished—no need to squander his limited cash making himself at home. He emptied the duffel bag onto the twin mattress: boots, jeans, and T-shirts. Sleeping bag. No computer, no cell phone, no expensive technology needed to maintain the simple life. The milk crate contained his small tent and other camping gear. The cooking utensils he had procured at the local Goodwill were housed in the kitchen at the Moonflower Motel, southeastern Utah's premier youth hostel, a mere ten yards away.

Even at 6:00 p.m. it was hotter in the trailer than it was outside. It was the beginning of August, and two minutes in the dry desert heat made him slick with sweat. He appreciated that the Moonflower had a swamp cooler, an energy-efficient device that used a pan of water and a fan instead of the environmentally egregious Freon used in the air conditioners of the Northeast. The swamp cooler only reduced the heat by twenty degrees, but that was better than nothing.

Luke shoved his stuff to one side and sat down on the bed, taking in the compactness of the room. It would be nice not to live out of his duffel bag, the way he had for the past eight months. During that time he had become part of the fabric of the youth hostel through hard work and loyalty to the owners, Jim and Clare. Now he had a salary and a place of his own, rent-free. He must have looked odd, coming in two days after Christmas, alone. He had been flying on adrenaline, sixteen, technically a runaway. He had rented a bunk in one of the dorm rooms for a night, a week, and then started doing cleaning and grunt work for Jim in exchange for the bed, the constant change of roommates reminding him of his transience.

His seventeenth birthday had passed in March without incident or acknowledgment. He couldn't believe how easy it was. People believed whatever he wanted them to. He could be as vague as he liked about where he was from and how old he was. Nobody seemed to mind vagueness in the Southwest. You could never be vague in New York City—too many people asked questions. You always had to *be* something. In New York, he wanted to be a painter, but he hadn't picked up a brush in over a year. In Moab, he was just Luke.

"Knock, knock." He heard a voice call out and the heavy tread of footsteps crunching the gravel. He smiled: there was Jim, towering in the doorway. "Everything to your satisfaction? Wow, I can't even fit in here!" Luke watched Jim unwedge himself and step outside, where Luke joined him. "I'm glad that Clare suggested you move out of the dorm rooms so you could have more privacy," Jim said.

"It's just what I need," Luke said. "I'll finish unpacking and get to work, don't worry."

Jim wiggled his eyebrows. "Me, worry? I left my worries behind in Ohio."

"I wonder what it's like to be able to do that."

"Life is too serious to be taken seriously," Jim said gravely, and then winked. "But it might be a good idea to change your shirt." Jim chuckled as he crossed over to the hostel building that he had painted a light blue. It looked almost garish in the sunlight compared with the rustic wood stain that was left on the picnic tables in front and the surrounding cabins.

Luke glanced down at his shirt, now drenched in sweat. He pulled it off as he stepped back up into the trailer. He leaned against the wall and studied the painting. It was two feet by four feet and had hung in the living room of his family's apartment for over ten years. His mother, Georgia, had painted it from a photograph she had taken of him when he was five, standing on a rock in the Fiery Furnace area of nearby Arches National Park. The portrait was ablaze with oranges, reds, and yellows streaming out of Luke's dark brown hair, and his face was upturned and smiling at the light. Georgia's love for him was in those brushstrokes, and he needed to have that reminder that once upon a time someone had believed in him.

He blinked his eyes and appraised his new home again. The bed was in the corner with drawers underneath for his clothes, and there were a couple of chairs and a table for eating-drawing-reading. There was no running water in the trailer—no sink, toilet, or shower. A separate building with showers was available for those who weren't staying in the main hostel but in trailers, cabins, or tents.

Luke felt something like excitement for the first time in almost a year, and he welcomed it. He could hear the murmur of voices and laughter outside. Guests were returning from their day trips to nearby parks—Arches, Canyonlands, Monument Valley—and he needed to get back to the hostel. He stashed his stuff and put on a clean shirt, then jumped out the door and locked it, pocketing the key. He looked to the La Sal Mountains in the distance. He felt both contained and free in this valley, surrounded by the red sandstone of the Moab Rim. Moab was named after the Promised Land, he remembered Jim saying during one of their many conversations that winter, a twinkle in his eye. The first Mormons had given the town its biblical name in 1880.

It had certainly been that for Jim and Clare, discovering Moab last summer on a meandering road trip through the Southwest, after taking their daughter, Ava, to New York following her high school graduation in May.

"Where in New York?" Luke had asked.

"She goes to Barnard College, on the Upper West Side," Jim had told him.

"She must be crazy smart," Luke had said, not mentioning that he'd lived around the corner from the school.

"Well, she was smart enough to want to get a job right away, rather than tour the country with her parents." Jim and Clare had burned rubber in a straight line west from New York to Denver and started their wanderings there. At first they just enjoyed the sights, but when they got to Moab, they were amazed by their visceral response to the place, and their willingness to jump into another life. Some would call it impulsive, but Luke knew exactly how Jim and Clare felt, although he didn't consider it a "spiritual conversion" the way they did. Well, the way Jim did.

A cherry red Jeep was idling in front of the hostel. The main parking lot must be full.

"Can I help you?" Luke asked, approaching it.

"Yeah." There were two college-age kids in the Jeep. "We just got here. Where can we park?" Luke directed them to the alternate parking area behind his trailer.

He nodded to a few travelers congregating out front by the picnic tables as he opened the door to the hostel, knowing he would find Tangerine inside. She had jumped at the chance to fill in for him at the front desk because she was looking for more hours to work so that she could afford to stay longer. It was toward the end of the season, and businesses weren't hiring anymore. She was talking to Brigitte from Chicago, who also had started living at the hostel earlier this summer and was thinking about quitting law school. Brigitte had patched together a full-time work schedule by cleaning at the hostel and making mochas at the coffeehouse on Center Street.

Luke stopped, mesmerized by Tangerine's Australian twang. She had very bright red hair in two braids down her back, green eyes, a nose ring, a tongue stud, and several earrings. For all of that outer adornment, she didn't wear any makeup, and Luke thought she was stunning. Of course, she also made him nervous. Luke grabbed the guest book from the desk, wanting to finish the paperwork from his busy shift.

"I'm broke and my mum wants me to come home, but I'm not ready to leave." Tangerine sounded unusually glum, and the intimacy in her sadness made Luke feel like an intruder, so he turned and went back outside.

The sun was finally behind the building, and guests were milling about, wondering what to do for dinner. One family was firing up one of the grills, and two of the three picnic tables were full. It was virtually impossible to be alone at the hostel, and Luke had to zigzag between three children playing tag to get to the empty picnic table to finish his work. He saw the guys from the cherry red Jeep and motioned them toward the door, knowing that Tangerine would get them settled.

Hal sat down next to him. Hal had been hanging around the hostel for years, so when Jim bought the place and took over, he sort of adopted Hal with it, giving him the glorified title of "maintenance manager," which was a nice way of saying that Hal was willing to do the dirty work but needed some management himself. Hal lived in a trailer on the grounds, even though he had family in town. Luke had never gotten the whole story, but he knew that Hal had been born and raised in the area, that his geologic knowledge was impressive, and that he believed in the inherent evil of extraterrestrials and Bigfoot. He was also a diagnosed schizophrenic, but Georgia, who had been an art therapist specializing in adult psychosis, would have called Hal "high-functioning."

Luke raised his chin briefly. "How're ya doin'?" he asked. Luke noticed that Hal had food stuck in his drooping mustache, but it never did any good to call attention to that. His graying hair was also constantly a bird's nest, adding to his permanent look of confusion.

"Hangin' in there," Hal said as he turned away from Luke to greet the two new guys, who sat down at the other end of the table, opening cans of beer.

Hal started talking to them. "You know the Zettians come in and just explode your world, man. It's a totally mind-blowing experience!" The Zettians again. Luke smiled weakly at the new guys. He needed to do some damage control.

"That's cool, man," Luke said, knowing from experience that the best way to deal with Hal was to agree with him.

"No, man, it's not cool." Oops, wrong. "It's not cool to have aliens invade your head and take you away with them. Those negative vortexes, man, stay away from them."

"Wait," one of the guys said, trying not to laugh. "What's a negative vortex?"

Hal's eyes bugged out. "You don't know about vortexes? There's electric and magnetic, positive and negative. You've got to watch out for the negative. You don't know what can come through. Bigfoot, the Zettians. They take over your mind and you can't think for yourself, and the Zettians do whatever they want with you . . . They pick your brain, they just pick, pick, pick . . ."

"Hal," Luke said gently, putting his hand on Hal's arm. It always made him a little nervous when Hal was in one of his moods. "Sorry, man, that *is* rough. Hey, could you make sure there's enough toilet paper in the bathrooms? Somebody mentioned something about it this afternoon, but I forgot which one . . ." The look of panic was beginning to fade from Hal's face, and he nodded.

"I'll get right to it," he said, and went inside the hostel.

"Was he for real?" came the inevitable question, and the two guys laughed. Luke laughed too, and he relaxed. Some people thought Hal was scary, but he wasn't dangerous, just part of the wacky charm of the hostel. And he was definitely for real. At the Moonflower, Luke didn't have to question his reality, the way he'd been forced to last year in New York. He shook his head slightly. Home in New York with his father, Frank. That was another lifetime ago. Home could be anywhere. Home was right here. He loved this makeshift community.

Luke finished the paperwork and, hearing giggles at another table, looked up. When had Bruno come in with his harem? Bruno had taken a group of girls to Monument Valley for the day. He was a guest from San Francisco who kept prolonging his stay, one week turning into seven. He also apparently had unlimited means, because instead of looking for work, he was getting to know the area very well by touring around with whatever pretty faces happened by the Moonflower.

Luke smelled something delicious coming from Bruno's table and realized that he was starving. He stood up and went over to investigate. There was Dominique from Montreal, almost sitting in Bruno's lap as he held up a piece of Navajo bread smothered in honey.

9

And there was Jen, sitting aloof, trying to look as if she belonged. Jen was barely fourteen, and in the past couple of months had blossomed from an awkward eighth grader into a beauty with long chestnut hair.

"What a funny name!" Dominique was saying.

"What's a funny name?" Luke asked.

"Hey, buddy." Bruno gave Luke a nod. "Mexican Hat. It makes sense to me. Doesn't it look like a Mexican Hat to you?" Dominique shrugged. Mexican Hat was the name of a massive rock on the edge of Monument Valley that looked exactly like a sombrero. Luke sensed that Dominique would just be passing through. She wasn't that certain kind of person, like Tangerine, Brigitte, or even Bruno, who would become bewitched by the majesty of the red rocks and look for reasons to stay. Usually the spell would wear off after a few months and people would go back to their regular lives. That wouldn't happen to Luke, though. This was his regular life.

And it was Jen's too. She lived about half a mile away, and Clare had befriended her when she joined the mentoring program at the local school as a way to become part of the larger Moab community. Jen had even "run away" to the hostel once and begged Clare to adopt her, but Jim had called her parents, Bill and Kerri, and that was that. What was she doing here on a Friday night?

"Stopped by Café Esmeralda, huh?" Luke gazed longingly at the bread. "Good trip?"

Bruno looked up from his bread and winked. "Can't talk now, buddy. Gotta eat!"

"Bruno! You've got honey dripping down your chin!" Dominique squealed.

Luke rolled his eyes at Bruno and gave him a mock salute as he turned and went inside. Clare was now behind the desk.

"Ah! The guest book!" She beamed at him. "Tangerine checked

in two young men from Iowa." He handed the book to her, and she opened it, finding the right page immediately. "Tucker and Chris. Cabin 9. They're just staying for the night," she said, smoothing her brown hair behind her ear.

"Your friend is sitting outside," Luke said.

Clare glanced up at him. "My friend?"

"Jen."

"Oh dear," she said, and paused. "Can you finish this for me while I go see why she's here?"

"No problem," Luke said as he took Clare's place and she hurried out the door. He noticed that one of the wooden Kokopelli dolls made by Jim's Hopi friend Cha'tima had been sold. Jim was obsessed with Kokopelli, and even practiced carving little figurines of the deity himself in his woodshop behind the hostel. The hump-backed trickster playing the flute was the most popular symbol of the Southwest, representing the chasing away of sadness.

Luke wrote in the new guests' names and turned around to face the kitchen. On his left was a door that led upstairs to Clare and Jim's quarters, and to the right was a staircase that led to the dorm rooms. For now, he had the kitchen all to himself, unusual for this time of night. He could keep an eye on the desk while he made dinner. He opened the refrigerator and looked in his corner to see what he had left. Jim and Clare also kept a stocked canteen for guests, and Luke used it when he didn't have time to go to the grocery store.

There wasn't much choice: eggs, a few veggies, a tiny bit of cheddar, and a pork chop. Luke could have gone back outside and thrown the meat on a grill, but he liked the quiet of the kitchen. Besides, tomorrow Jim and Clare were having their monthly barbecue for the guests and workers. He would be in carnivore heaven. For now he decided to make an omelet. Tangerine came into the kitchen as he was whisking the eggs.

"'Ello, mate!" she exclaimed. The clouds had disappeared from her face. She banged around in the cupboards and turned around with a box of cereal that had a big T drawn on the front in marker. "Want some?"

"Huh? Oh, cereal for dinner? I'm okay, thanks. Making an omelet," Luke said as he watched Tangerine throw the box of cereal in the air and catch it again.

"Ugh. I don't see how you can cook in this heat."

"Heat, what heat?"

"Oh, he's using humor now, is he?" Tangerine elbowed him, and Luke turned back to chopping the mushrooms and half a green pepper. He didn't want her to see him blush. He felt her breath on the back of his neck as she peered over his shoulder. His mind was racing. What did a normal person say in this situation?

"You want some?" he asked.

"He finally gets it!" Her laugh was confident and loud. She backed away, and he heard her slide into a chair at the table. He cracked two more eggs into the bowl, whisking them all together. "We're going to try to get to Behind the Rocks for the moonrise again tonight," Tangerine said. "Wanna come?"

Tourists might flock to the national parks, but there was so much beauty in places where you didn't have to pay an entrance fee. Corona Arch, Portal Overlook, Fisher Towers, Hunter Canyon, Negro Bill Canyon, Angel Rock in Hidden Valley, and especially the Moab Rim, standing fortresslike for miles on the south side of town. Behind the Rocks was unofficially called Back of Beyond, beyond the Moab Rim, beyond Hidden Valley, "beyond your wildest dreams" according to some.

"Ah. Fresh blood in Tucker and Chris. They look game," Luke said to the vegetables as they sautéed in the pan. A Moonflower tradition was to initiate any willing tourist into the thrills of hiking by moon and starlight; usually he loved this, experiencing this wayward heaven with other people.

"Last night sucked," Luke said. They hadn't even made it that far up the rim because someone had been cajoled into coming who shouldn't have. Granted, it had been unusually windy, but this someone had bitched and moaned the whole way, making the group abandon their hike. Fortunately, the someone had left this morning and Luke had already forgotten his name.

"Yeah, Todd was a pain in the arse, but he's gone, and it's not last night anymore, is it?" Tangerine raised an eyebrow. She was hard to say no to, but he wanted to say no. He wanted to be alone in his new trailer home. Still, it was tempting. She was tempting. He didn't say anything as he poured the eggs into the pan. "I'm taking your silence as a yes, you know. I need a buddy. Brigitte spends all of her evenings with her boyfriend, Carlos, now. C'mon, be my buddy."

"Maybe," he managed to mumble. It was nice to be included, even though she probably would have acted the same way with anybody else in the kitchen.

The door to the hostel opened, and Luke looked up to see Clare come in with Jen trailing behind.

"He is so hot," Jen was saying. "His name is Jaime, and he's staying at the campgrounds on Kane Creek."

"With his parents?" Clare asked as she grabbed her keys from behind the desk.

"Well . . ." Jen said. Clare gave her a sharp look. "Yes, yes, with his parents, okay? Anyway, thanks for giving me a ride to the movie theater. And for calling my mom, I guess."

"You should always check in with your mom. And you're meeting Brandi, right?"

"Yeah. Then she'll give me a ride home," Jen said as she followed Clare back out again. So Jen was here to get a ride the four miles into town.

Tangerine yawned. "How long does your omelet take? I see you've got it on very low heat."

"I thought that all you Aussie farmers knew how to cook?"

"Moi? Not only do I cook but I milk cows, groom horses, slaughter chickens. I could make you a shepherd's pie that would put hair on your chest."

Bruno would have had a smart remark, but Luke turned his eyes back to the omelet. He put the grated cheese on top, found plates in the cupboard above the stove, split the omelet in half, and joined Tangerine at the table.

"Such service!" she said, and took a bite. "Ooooh. I love capsicum."

"Say what?"

"These green bits."

"Oh, pepper."

"You say tomato, I say tomahto."

The front door opened, and Luke heard Dominique titter, followed by the murmur of other voices.

"TV time," Bruno announced, and Dominique's laughter followed him into the large common room adjoining the kitchen, which had a television and several couches.

Tangerine rolled her eyes and said in a stage whisper, "He's a piece of work, isn't he?"

Luke smiled. "You weren't immune to the Bruno charm when he first got here, if I remember correctly."

"Yeah, well, I'm immune now. I have six brothers and have been trained to see through charming men."

Luke wanted to ask Tangerine about her brothers, but she kept talking. "I might be moving on anyhow." She took another bite of eggs. "This is really delicious. You cook all the time, don't you?"

Luke shrugged. "It's something I like to do."

"You can cook for me anytime! What do you think of Taos? I'm thinking of heading that way—the season lasts longer, and there must be more work there."

"New Mexico?" He started to answer but lost her attention when the front door opened again.

"Cin!" Tangerine exclaimed.

"Hey, Clementine, Cool Hand."

Cin stood there, tan from days in the sun, her red cowboy hat perched on top of a wet mess of hair. She held out two pints of Ben & Jerry's ice cream.

"Bad day?" Luke asked, almost laughing as she slammed the ice cream onto the table and collapsed into a chair. Her name, Cinnamon Sprite, Cin for short, sounded like a sickeningly sweet candy or a porn star, neither of which was an apt description of this sinewy, swarthy, tall, dreadlocked woman. She insisted that it was her given name, claiming that her mother had been eating cinnamon toast and drinking Sprite for breakfast when she went into labor. Cin had been Jim and Clare's only full-time employee besides Hal when Luke arrived at the Moonflower, and they had developed an easy rapport. In the spring she had taken a job at Red Rock Rafting Tours and moved from the hostel into a used Airstream trailer that she parked off Kane Creek Road, near the Colorado River, leaving Luke to fill her shoes.

He had never seen anyone like her: she was from Kansas and as earthy as the desert itself, covered from head to toe in tattoos. Word was that she was a shaman, a healer who walked between this world and the "other" one that the airy-fairy types in Moab were looking for, but Luke didn't think of her that way. She was too strong and levelheaded. She took her hat off and put her head on the table, groaning.

"I need a little of my friends Ben and Jerry, a little of you two, and some mind-numbing TV. Is *Survivor* on by any chance?"

"The ridiculous is always on somewhere," Luke said. "Want some real food first? I can make some more."

Cin shook her head. "Sugar me up for now. And yes, I had a crappy day. Would you get the bowls? Can you stand listening to me complain for five minutes?"

"You? This should be interesting. Go ahead, be a venting machine," Luke said.

Tangerine cleared the table and brought back bowls and spoons. "Thanks," Cin said, and took a deep breath, closing her eyes. Then she opened them and started muscling the ice cream into the bowls.

"I'll come right to the point. I need help. Macleod put me in charge while he's gone on vacation for August, and then out of the blue, the office assistant decides to quit. Today!" She handed Luke a bowl, then Tangerine. "Anyone come around here looking for a few weeks of work?"

Tangerine stared at Cin.

"Hey, Tange," Luke said. "I know that there's not enough work at the Moonflower to keep you going, but would doing something like this be reason enough to stick around?"

"You thinking of bailing on us then?" Cin asked. Luke found himself hoping desperately that Tangerine would take the job. "Well, whoever I take on should know that there wouldn't be official training. I need help in the office, and with rigging and derigging the boats."

"Tange, this is the perfect solution, and you know it. Cin, she was just talking about going to Taos to look for a job."

"Oh, Clementine. Taos is fine for a visit now and then, but it ain't no Moab."

Cin had nicknames for everyone. Luke could count on his fingers the times he'd heard her call people by their given names. He had been very confused when she'd started calling him Cool Hand. The connection was *Cool Hand Luke*, a great movie starring Paul Newman, about prisoners working on a chain gang. Cin made Luke watch it with her, and he was honored by the nickname. Was he as likable, as determined as Paul Newman was in the movie? Tangerine was called Clementine he guessed for the citrus connection. Jim was Jesse for Jesse James, and Clare was Clarity Jane, instead of Calamity Jane.

Cin had also been on her own since she was sixteen. Luke didn't know all the details, except that she claimed to have run away with a circus and started her tattoo addiction there. Luke had gone with her to Albuquerque three months ago to see her get her latest one, which glistened green on her lower arm. A lizard. "A fat, lazy lizard. Helps the blackbird with my lucid dreaming," Cin had told him. Whatever that meant. He knew that her tattoos were very real to her. They were all different animals she said she'd met. She'd even named them.

"Is there any more ice cream?" Luke asked, and Cin pushed the empty pints over to him.

"Sorry, Cool Hand. So what about it, Clem? Why don't you try it out, come in for a few hours tomorrow?"

"Yes!"

"Good. Let's see what's on the boob tube."

Tangerine threw back her head and laughed. "I was going to bail. I can't believe it!" Luke stood up and stacked the bowls. "Oh, I'll wash up!" she offered, so he followed Cin into the TV lounge, where a crowd was watching *Survivor*. It was a particularly cruel episode.

"Ugh, this is too much." Cin closed her eyes.

"It's celebreality, baby," Luke said, smiling.

"It's humiliating, honey. And I thought this would be comforting!"

"They should be filming the Moonflower. Never a dull moment here," Tangerine joked from the doorway.

"True. But don't you think that people could use some more dull moments?" Cin got up and stretched. "Speaking of which, I could use some myself. Good night. See you tomorrow."

"Yeah, barbecue time," Luke said.

"Oh, see you there." Cin opened the door. "Hey, Clem, does ten a.m. work for you?"

"Yes, ma'am!" Tangerine said.

"It's time for Behind the Rocks!" Bruno hollered. The show was over.

"C'mon, Luke," Tangerine beckoned. Dull moments. Never. "C'mon. Please come out with us . . ."

• • •

Tangerine and Luke climbed into the bed of Bruno's truck along with Hal, Chris, and Tucker, while Dominique rode up front. They screeched down Kane Creek Road and parked underneath a ten-story-tall rock. Where was the secret entrance? It was as if the rocks shifted shape from day to night: what was obvious in the light was obscured by the dark. This was one of the things Luke loved about hiking at night. Bruno was the first to disappear into the crevice, Dominique right behind him.

"Wait, where did they go?" Tucker asked.

"Follow me," Tangerine said mysteriously.

"Oh, I see now." Tucker followed Tangerine. Chris went next, and Hal and Luke brought up the rear. Much of Luke's knowledge of the terrain was from taking these hikes with Hal.

Luke felt the support of the red earth as he put his right foot on a crag, holding on to the rock above him with his left hand, up, up, and up.

"Hey, watch out!" he heard Hal call as some rocks came tumbling down, barely missing Luke's head. "Be careful! This crypto soil isn't just weeds. It's live organic matter." Part of the initiation process for the newcomers would inevitably be a tutorial from Hal on how to treat the earth. Luke was always careful about where he put his feet, and he didn't want to step on any of the sparse vegetation: tufts of brush sprouting miraculously from seemingly solid rock.

His heart beat faster once he got to the top of the first precipice, where Tangerine and Hal were waiting for him. Thirty yards ahead were the others, looking like they were scaling another wall.

Luke heard Hal mutter "Useless" as they watched Tucker and Chris scramble up the rocks, dislodging a few.

Tangerine elbowed Luke and laughed softly. "Too bad we can't ditch him, but we're in it now," she whispered. "It will all be worth it once we get up to the top. Don't you want to hear Dominique squeal with delight?"

"No comment."

At the zenith, a flat expanse of mesa awaited them. The true area called Behind the Rocks was another four miles ahead, but this was usually as far as they went. Luke collapsed on the sandstone with the others, breathless from exertion. He could stare at the night sky forever. He tried to shut out the conversation around him: How many galaxies were there? How many universes? The chatter was giving him a headache.

He heard Tucker say, "We've got an apple and some super good weed. Any takers?"

Luke sat up. All eyes were on Tucker, who had the weed, and Chris, who had the apple. Luke kept quiet and watched Chris make a pipe out of the apple. The physics were bewildering: Three holes were needed to make an air chamber inside. When Chris finished, he gave the apple to Tucker, who put pot in one of the holes and then lit it, inhaling deeply. He gestured to Luke. Why not? He'd only smoked pot once before, with Hal, and hadn't been impressed, but what was the harm in trying again? He took the apple and the lighter and put his mouth over the hole as he had seen Tucker do, lighting the weed and breathing in slowly, imagining his lungs filling with THC. It seemed to go on forever, but at the very end of his breath, he felt as if something snagged in his chest, and he pulled the apple away, coughing violently.

"Oh, dude, you are going to be so stoned!" Was it Tucker who said that? Luke couldn't talk and he couldn't breathe. Why had he smoked? Why did he come out tonight? Tangerine was patting his back, and although it felt really good, he felt dwarfed by everything else. She didn't take the apple. Did he matter to anybody? Look at how his thoughts were floating around. He didn't like floating. He watched Dominique put her lips on the apple.

Hal also smoked and was wandering around muttering to himself. Hal was very conscientious about cleaning up after people, but this time he was angry about it. People would make fire pits out of smaller rocks and leave the garbage and ash, ignoring the credo around Moab to take out whatever you take in. Now Hal was throwing rocks, which was unlike him.

"No wonder everything is eroding," he yelled.

Uh-oh, Luke thought. *I should get up, shouldn't I?* But he couldn't move. He watched Bruno walk over to Hal with a "What's up, buddy?" and put an arm around his back.

"This will bring Bigfoot," Hal said accusingly, pointing at the rocks.

"Okay, dude. Bigfoot. No problem," Bruno said.

"No problem? How can you say no problem? Bigfoot is a problem, my friend."

Luke lay back on the rocks and half listened to Hal's tirade. He almost knew it by heart.

"I think we'd better go down and take him back." Bruno was standing over Luke.

"Can we sleep out here tonight?" Dominique asked in a dreamy voice. She looked like a pile of jelly. It wasn't a bad idea, but someone had to take Hal back.

"I don't think so. Look at him." Bruno pointed to Hal, who was sitting with his head down and his arms wrapped around his knees. "Let's go. Party's over."

"Oh, man, that was some strong stuff. I can't move!" Dominique groaned.

Tangerine jumped up. "Dominique doesn't look so good, Bruno. How are we going to get her and Hal down the rocks?"

Luke saw Bruno look at Dominique with contempt.

"Let's get her up and walk her around. C'mon, Dom." Bruno pulled Dominique to her feet.

I should help her. If I move around, I'll feel better too, Luke thought, and he slowly got up and saw Dominique put her arms around Bruno and try to kiss him. It was painful to watch: Bruno standing like a statue, staring off into space.

"What's the rush, dude? It will wear off in a little while, and we can go down then," Tucker said, sitting with Chris, oblivious.

Bruno's eyes shot daggers. "I have to take Hal and Dominique back, so if you want a ride, come now." He gestured to Luke. "Help me with her." Luke came over to put an arm around Dominique, whose body was vibrating with giggles. They walked her toward the path, and for a while she was compliant, but then she lifted her legs and gave them all her weight. Bruno let go, she fell, and Luke fell on top of her.

"Owwww!" Dominique screamed.

That was embarrassing, Luke thought as he took the hand that Tangerine offered to help him up.

"I've never known you to smoke pot," Tangerine teased. Luke couldn't think of anything to say. He didn't want her to let go of his hand, it felt so good. But even stoned, he couldn't be so bold as to tighten his grip, and he let her hand drop to her side.

• • •

Getting the rest of the way back down the rocks had not been fun, he and Bruno taking turns carrying and cajoling Dominique. Fortunately, Hal had chilled out and made it down himself. Tangerine had been in high spirits and had taken Bruno's car keys and driven them back to the hostel. It was just after midnight when they returned. Luke had gone straight to the trailer after telling everyone good night.

Now he lay in bed, thinking. Dominique, Tangerine, Georgia. Sometimes mind-wandering could be a good thing, sometimes not. He shook his head; he didn't want to think about Georgia. Was he still stoned? He stared at the painting for a minute, and then it came to him—the kachina doll.

When he lived in New York, the kachina doll had sat at the foot of his bed. As he got older, he sometimes thought that this was silly, but he and Georgia had always laughed together about it, so he kept it there. Maybe it was having his own place that made him want to have his doll at the foot of his bed. Where was it? He remembered stuffing it in his backpack when he left New York, but he had never unpacked it. He got up and found his backpack by the door. The kachina was at the bottom of the front pocket, and he sat back down on the bed and looked at it, remembering.

It must have been the summer he was six. It was the second time that he and his parents had vacationed in Moab. They had spent the day exploring the Navajo reservation in Monument Valley. Afterward, they'd checked out the smattering of tourist shops. In one of the shops, they had been fascinated by a life-size kachina with a bear's face. "A true work of art," Georgia had whispered, looking at the price tag. "Worth more than four thousand dollars, I'd say."

The shopkeeper had nodded. "This kachina was carved by an artisan in our neighboring Hopi tribe. Do you know about kachinas? Kachinas are the Hopi religious icons, teaching symbols. The Hopi carve kachinas to represent every aspect of their mythology, be it animal, vegetable, mineral . . . ancestral. I will show you some smaller, more affordable imitations." He had brought them over to a bookshelf filled with hundreds of small dolls. Luke had been entranced, listening to the shopkeeper's lesson on kachinas.

"During religious ceremonies, people wear masks and, through dancing and music, become one with their kachina, celebrating life and praying for a good harvest. These dolls embody the spirits of those dancers."

Luke had picked a doll with a bear's head and a body carved out of a soft wood, wearing a red leather skirt. The shopkeeper had told them that the bear kachina is the healer. "She is one of the strongest, for she can heal the sick."

Georgia had bought it for him, and together they had named her Ursula. "It means 'little bear' in Latin," Georgia had explained. The kachina doll was a part of Georgia, just as the painting was, and he wanted part of her with him. He realized that he *wanted* to be thinking about her. It was okay.

Memories of Georgia made him want to go up to Angel Rock and lie on the rocks and count the stars, to be even more alone than he felt in his trailer. Angel Rock had been her favorite, and he appreciated that it was probably because it was a hike Luke could manage as a small child. If you walked past Angel Rock, you would find Hidden Valley, and then Behind the Rocks.

He could walk from the Moonflower to Angel Rock in twenty minutes.

His fingers smoothed over the rugged construction of the doll: the red leather covering some of the wood, brown fur on the back of the head, and the strange face, meticulously carved. The turquoise eyes were loose and probably needed to be glued back on. He remembered the hope and encouragement that Ursula had always given him, there on the foot of his bed. But that was long ago, and he didn't want to let himself get too sentimental. Still, he put her in her place, opened the door to his trailer, and began walking toward Angel Rock.

. . .

This part of the Moab Rim was a bit lower than on Kane Creek Road, so climbing the tiers of rock seemed effortless compared with earlier that night. He hiked higher and higher until he saw the mesa and the rock formation he had been looking for. And smoke. Smoke?

Was there a fire? There was smoke billowing over Angel Rock. Instead of walking straight to the top, he veered to the side to better assess the situation.

Luke saw a large figure cloaked head to toe in brown fur. Luke was sweating in just a T-shirt. What was going on? His mind flashed to Hal's Bigfoot. He watched the back of the figure—was it a man? A woman? A woman couldn't be that big. Probably a man. He snuck a little closer. It was tourist season; it was bound to be some hippie-dippie tourist, thinking that this mesa was a center of spiritual energy and praying to whatever gods might be listening.

Luke started to get agitated just thinking about that. He decided to go another way. He snuck one last look—but there was no fire, no fur-man. Nothing. That was impossible. Luke had been watching the figure for nearly two minutes.

He jumped over the rock and strode across the mesa to the spot where the fire had been. But there was no small circle of rocks, no ashes, no burn marks, just pure, unadulterated red sandstone. Bigfoot traveling through dimensions? That was ridiculous. He was losing his mind. Or was it the pot?

Luke sat on his knees, feeling the earth for a sign, anxiety rising in his throat. The flat surface was cool beneath him. Then he swung his legs out in front of him and collapsed back, stretching his arms overhead. Looking up, he saw a shooting star. He tried to concentrate on the stars and empty his thoughts. But it wasn't working; he was positive that there had been somebody right here, right where he was lying. He closed his eyes and must have dozed, then woke with a start when he felt someone stroking his hair. He looked up into a pair of brown eyes, and for a moment he saw Georgia. But as his eyes focused, he saw that he was looking into the eyes of someone else. Who was it? What was it? A bear. A big brown bear. Instead of being afraid, he almost smiled.

You see, Hal? There's no Bigfoot, no bogeyman . . . it's just a sweet bear . . . His eyes closed again, and he fell back asleep.

• • •

"Luke! Where are you?" His mother was calling him. Luke was giggling, hiding behind a giant red stone. They had been hiking the

Slickrock Trail at the Sand Flats Recreation Area, where there weren't many boulders like this. He loved this game.

"Luke!" Maybe he should give his mother a hint. She sounded like she might give up, and he wanted her to play.

"You'll never find me!" He wanted to climb up the boulder. Luckily, there were lots of little rocks around it that he could use to help him shimmy up this one. He found that his hands could grip easily.

"Mommy!" he yelled at the top. Georgia was sitting with Frank, looking in the opposite direction. She turned around and waved at him, beaming.

Frank got up and walked toward him, arms outstretched. "Free fall, Luke!" Luke felt exhilarated. Hiding, climbing, falling. He took a deep breath and catapulted himself into Frank's arms.

They hiked back to their campsite, Luke riding on Frank's shoulders. He had never slept in a tent, and he was overflowing with excitement. After dinner, they snuggled in their sleeping bags, and Luke said, "Tell me again . . ." Luke loved hearing the story of how Frank and Georgia met.

"We met right here, pumpkin, in Moab," Georgia started. "On the Slickrock Trail, where we were today. I was on my mountain bike when I saw this man on the ground. The earth here is perfect for mountain biking—"

"If you know what you're doing!" Frank continued, looking at Georgia. "I had no clue. One minute I'm up and having fun, then I hit the path in the wrong way and *boom!* I'm down. But who knows what would have happened if I hadn't fallen?"

"His friend had just left him in the dust! So I stopped. And once we realized that we both lived in New York, on the Upper West Side, well, we were inseparable."

"Our meeting was kismet," Frank said.

"Kismet," Georgia agreed.

How Luke missed Frank! But Frank might as well have died with Georgia.

.   .   .

Luke opened his eyes, and he was alone.

What had just happened? He crawled back down to steady earth and reality, made his way to his trailer, and fell into his soft bed and a deep, normal sleep.

saturday

two

"Hi. My name is Frank, and I'm an alcoholic."

"Hi, Frank," said the room full of people, including Ava. She felt hot in the little space, and the air conditioner wasn't doing its job. August heat in New York City was just unbearable, and sweat was oozing from everybody's pores. *We all stink.* She didn't know if she could stay in this room much longer. She wished that she had gone to the gym instead, where there was AC and she could regulate her own sweat. She glanced at the time on her iPod. It was 9:15 a.m. and she had another forty-five minutes before she could go somewhere else. Home to sleep for another hour or two, if she was lucky. Here she was, at an AA meeting on a Saturday morning. Ava was only eighteen and by far the youngest person in the room. Everyone else her age was trying to sleep through a hangover, right? At least she had woken up in her own bed, knowing what she did last night. And what had she done? Worked at the Living Room Lounge until midnight, and then gone home to struggle with insomnia. Pathetic. She was hungover from not sleeping.

She looked down at her sunburnt legs and thought, *Too flabby.* She caught herself banging her knees together and stopped. Nerves. She glanced around the room. There was a table for some to sit around and more chairs against the walls. Ava never liked to sit at the table, because everyone would look at her. She was sitting in the corner with her back to the wall, facing the front door, and had already tuned out the drunk who was talking. He had come in with Charlie, who was sitting next to her. She closed her eyes and tried to focus on listening. *Let go,* she commanded herself. *Let go of all these negative thoughts.*

She had listened to Louise tell her "story": what it was like (drinking), what happened (getting sober), and what it's like now (staying sober). Talking in AA meetings was called "sharing." She supposed that Frank was sharing either how he related to Louise's story or his own story, which was what people did in meetings, but her monkey mind was doing gymnastics. Louise had said something about having to get out of her own way in order to get sober and be happy. She was the chief cause of her unhappiness. Alcohol was but a symptom of her problems. She also talked about having a genetic predisposition, a history of alcoholism in her family. There was an alcohol gene? Like whether you had brown eyes or blue? Ava looked exactly like her dad, tall, blue-eyed, and blond. *He* wasn't an alcoholic, but his father was. So there you had it.

She tuned back in to the man's words. Frank's words.

"I chose alcohol over my son, over my life, so I put him in the position of having to run away from me eight months ago. But that wasn't my wake-up call. I was glad he was gone so that I didn't have to see the disappointment, the disgust on his face. I had been sober his whole life—he had never seen me drunk! But the progression of this disease . . . The spiritual, physical, and emotional damage it has inflicted, I have inflicted on myself, on him . . . But I haven't had a drink yet today. I don't know how I'm here now, but I'm here, and I have a sliver of willingness to get sober to be worthy of my son again."

Frank went on to talk about his wife having been killed in a car crash and how he blamed himself, because if they hadn't argued for so long, she wouldn't have had to take a cab to work. So he started drinking again because G-O-D had reneged on the life he had given him. What did that mean? Ava felt a chill in the sweaty room. She had started drinking when Nana was dying. Was that the same thing?

Frank had stopped talking, and hands were raised. Not hers.

"I drank to get drunk; I loved it." Julia was speaking now. "I drank for any reason, any occasion: celebrations, breakups, any kind of stress, doing well at work, getting fired. I drank to mask my feelings, especially anger. And now I'm learning *not* to drink for any reason, to deal with my feelings . . ."

Ava still didn't know how to deal with her feelings, but something about AA was working for her. She had managed to stay sober for fifty-eight days, which she hadn't been able to do since she started drinking in earnest her junior year of high school. What a short and pathetic drinking career. If only she had paced herself, and not spun out of control.

Ava looked at all the little AA platitudes on the wall. "Let go and let God," one said. Whatever that meant. She wasn't sure about this God stuff. Someone had told her that a better way to say it was "Let go or be dragged." But how? How do you let go? Her favorite AA saying was "Son of a bitch, everything's real," or S.O.B.E.R., but they didn't have a plaque for that one. Her skin tingled. The fact that she was sitting in this room was surreal beyond belief. The lingo was hokey, and there was nothing as dated as the AA literature. The Big Book, copies for sale on the table, was called so for anonymity purposes and was the cornerstone of Alcoholics Anonymous, explaining "How It Works." It was written in the 1930s by a bunch of men! The title made it sound like a book for a secret society, and the language was so antiquated, it was either almost cute or a huge turn-off, depending on her mood.

Charlie had introduced himself to her after one of her first meetings, and she had recognized him from an episode of *Will & Grace* in which he played a guy dating Will. The first few weeks she'd struggled with whether AA was for her or not, but every time she came to this room, she looked forward to seeing Charlie. He always smiled at her and made her feel welcome, and not like a loser. She had wondered if he was gay; after hearing him share a few times it became clear that he was. He was a good-looking guy in his thirties, successful, able to articulate his emotions, warm, drop-dead gorgeous. In other words, he blew her stereotyping of alcoholics out of the water.

"What, are we all supposed to be old men in raincoats?" Charlie had asked her. She had to admit that was her general idea. "Let me tell you something, sweets, everybody, alcoholic or not, has problems. *We're* lucky that we have a solution." It was strongly suggested that people new to AA get someone who'd been through the ropes to be their sponsor, help them with the Big Book and with the steps. The *twelve* steps. It took Ava a month to muster up the courage to ask Charlie. He happened to be in between jobs and was happy to take her under his wing.

The guy who had shared about his son had walked in with Charlie. Were they friends? Frank had four days . . . back. That meant he had been sober before, then started drinking again. Ava focused on the meeting. People were raising their hands again, but her arms felt like lead. She wasn't used to sharing much about herself, but Charlie had been urging her to do so. "We get sober in public," he had told her.

"Hi, my name is Charlie, and I'm an alcoholic."

"Hi, Charlie." He always shared about gratitude. Sometimes it was a little nauseating. He shared about being "grateful" that Frank was there . . . *Frank* used to be Charlie's sponsor? Grateful for the support he continued to feel from a mix of complete strangers, a random subway car full of people, successful and not, young and not, a place that transcended race, age, economics, politics, gender, and sexuality.

When Charlie was finished, he reached over and raised Ava's hand. "What the . . . ?" And she was picked to share. "Hi, I'm Ava, and I'm an alcoholic. I guess I'm sharing." There was laughter, and she caught a wink from Charlie. "It's so hot in here, I can barely concentrate. Yeah, I get in my own way a lot. I suck at listening, but that sentence stuck with me . . . My mood has vacillated so many times in the past half hour, I wonder if I'm mentally ill." People laughed in an understanding way, and Charlie smiled encouragingly at her.

"I know intellectually that I'm better off trying to relate to the feelings of other alcoholics rather than the facts, but I still wonder if I'm too young to be a real one. It's really hard to go out with my friends and not drink. In fact, I can't even do that. So I'm lonely and feel like a loser. I went bananas last year. Freshman in college, in New York City, away from family . . . How could I have gotten so crazy?

"I started drinking three years ago, when my nana was diagnosed with throat cancer. My parents took care of her, and what did I do? I checked out. My mom was an ER nurse when she wasn't at Nana's bedside, trying to be strong, and my dad was distracted, trying to take care of both of them. As long as I kept my grades up, I thought I could get away with anything. And look, I got into Barnard, so nothing is wrong with me, right?" Ava paused. "But then I almost flunked out. And I thought I was so smart. Different, you know?

"Nana was my real parent, and now she's dead. Anyway, after my nana died, it dawned on my parents that not only did they have a daughter but they didn't know what to do with one. And believe me, I used that to my advantage. None of us knew how to deal with each other, and all I wanted to do was drink, and find the next party. What was it Julia said about anger? Drinking to mask that? I never thought I was angry before. That was an emotion I didn't understand. I was sweet! And deeply depressed. I read in a psychology book that depression is anger turned inward. That blew my mind.

"So I *am* angry. I feel angry at my parents for moving on, at Nana for dying . . . and I feel so angry that alcohol doesn't work anymore, that I have to come here." More laughter in the room. "Sorry, guys, but that's the way I feel. And it's like I've lost my grandmother all over again, like I've lost my best friend." Her mind went blank and her voice trailed off as she ran out of steam, finishing with a mumbled "Anyway, thanks for letting me share."

She felt as if bright lights had been turned on her and flushed crimson, but already the next person had started sharing. She looked around the room and let her eyes rest on Frank, who was staring at her. She looked away and squirmed, then looked back to see if he was still staring. Fortunately, he wasn't. He was older. Fifty? Tall and very skinny. Gaunt really. Unshaven. An Al Pacino look-alike who had seen better days. Frank did not look healthy. He looked like he had been through hell.

Would she look that way if she didn't stay sober?

Monkey mind, all over the place. Charlie said that extreme distraction was "normal" in early sobriety, and that she would become more focused.

She hadn't been able to listen to her mother's reasons for moving. Great, you guys want to be more creative? How was running a youth hostel in the middle of nowhere achieving that? Jim carving Hopi gods out of wood was a stupid hobby. Clare writing poetry was ridiculous. Wow, her thoughts were really mean-spirited. She was a mean, bad, angry person, and she wanted that person to disappear. She had tried to drink her away. She knew that she couldn't talk to her parents without sounding like a raving lunatic, so she didn't return their calls.

People were standing up to say the Serenity Prayer that ended each meeting. She stood up and held Charlie's hand and that of the woman on her other side.

God, grant me the serenity to accept the things I cannot change, the courage to change the things I can, and the wisdom to know the difference. Acceptance, courage, wisdom. She had none of these things yet, and she needed them desperately.

three

Luke awoke to sunlight glaring down on him through the tiny window and checked his watch: 8:47 a.m. Good, he hadn't totally overslept: he had to relieve Jim of desk duty in thirteen minutes. He sat up and saw the doll. The bear—no. He was determined to put last night out of his mind. Luke had become a person who didn't believe in anything but the concrete. Smoking pot and looking at the kachina doll had tricked him into seeing things up at Angel Rock. He put the doll behind some books. He would forget about it. He quickly got dressed, a Coldplay T-shirt tucked into his jeans with a belt. Casual but formal. That was Luke.

He was distracted as he interacted with the guests and the staff. He checked people out, including Chris and Tucker, and gave folks advice on where the best hikes were. Brigitte and Tangerine cleaned rooms until 9:45, and then Brigitte gave Tangerine a ride to Red Rock Rafting on her way to work at the coffeehouse. Hal was mopping the same spot on the floor in front of the desk over and over again.

Luke wondered if Hal had been doing moonflower, and if he had slept at all. Hal was addicted to moonflower and marijuana. Moonflowers bloomed at night and died in the morning, blooming again after the sun set. "On the verge of death, they become transformational," Hal had told Luke in his most reverent voice. In other words, they were hallucinogenic. Hal had confided to Luke that he was supposed to take medicine but that naturally occurring moonflower and pot were the only medications he would use, the only ones that made him feel normal, that worked. Moonflower was also poisonous. "But so glorious, white petals unfolding in the moonlight." Hal could wax poetic, but Luke was never tempted to try it himself.

"Moonflower morning, Hal?" Luke gently asked.

"Huh? No, no . . . not moonflower . . . just thinking I guess is all."

"That spot looks great. Why don't you vacuum the common room now?" Hal was nothing if not diligent. A good worker. Maybe drugs did help him to function. Who was Luke to judge?

• • •

The morning flew by with all the comings and goings. Bruno took off with some guests to the watering hole in Mill Creek. Dominique came down later with her bags, looking puffy-eyed.

"Hi there. You okay? I thought you were leaving tomorrow," Luke said.

Dominique gave a halfhearted laugh and looked away. "Change of plans," she mumbled as she handed him her credit card. He felt almost embarrassed for her. After Dominique left he enjoyed two minutes of silence before he heard Jim's feet coming down the stairs.

"Hey, buddy, can I send you on a couple of errands?" Luke nodded as Jim gave him his car keys, a piece of paper, and cash. "Oh, I forgot to put soda on there." Luke read the long list. It looked like the canteen was nearly empty, and they needed groceries for the barbecue too.

Luke walked along the path to the green Bronco, picking up cigarette butts and throwing them into the obvious garbage can at the foot of the driveway. It didn't bother him today; usually the insensitivity of the guests irritated him, the hypocrisy of coming to revel in the earth's glory only to use it as a garbage dump. But his anger and confusion had disappeared. He felt clear. Work was good that way.

He gave himself a half smile in the tinted windows of the Bronco and noticed that his wavy brown hair was getting too long. He opened the car door and sat down, lovingly touching the wheel. Jim was a great friend.

Luke had gotten his driver's license in June. Jim had been the one to insist he learn how to drive back in March and had volunteered to teach him. He couldn't say no.

Jim had been whistling something hauntingly familiar the first time he had taken Luke out to an empty parking lot for a driving lesson. It had made Luke think of home and he had been surprised to find his eyes smarting. What was it? "Fly me to the moon," Jim had started singing, "and let me play among the stars . . ."

Julie London? Luke would have expected this blond, shaggy mountain of a man to be belting out Led Zeppelin or something along those lines, not Julie. Georgia used to listen to that old-style kind of stuff when she was painting or cooking. His eyes were burning. He had never been able to cry about Georgia; emotion stuck in his heart. She *was* his heart. Luke tried not to think about the past, or about the future for that matter. But at that moment in the Bronco, it had all melted down his cheeks, memories of the last time he had seen her.

• • •

"Hey, Mom!" Luke called across the street. He had been waiting for her on Riverside Drive, humoring her need for time-with-my-son-I've-barely-seen-you-all-summer. Luke thought that they saw each other enough, but it was important to Georgia that they spend quality time together outside of passing each other in the kitchen.

Georgia's face lit up when she saw him. "Oh, thanks for meeting me!" She had her Rollerblades slung over one shoulder. "Come on. Time's a-wastin'." She was six feet tall with shoulder-length brown hair that she dyed red, and she was wearing cut-off jeans and a T-shirt. They started walking down the steps and into the park. "How was your first day of school?"

My God, she's such a dork, Luke thought, but found himself smiling too. School had been crazy. He had finally been able to transfer into LaGuardia High School for his junior year, based on his art portfolio. It was a dream come true.

"I'm still pinching myself." They sat down on a bench and put on their Rollerblades. "I'm so glad that I kept reapplying. I feel like I will get to do art all day long."

"I am so proud of you! Persistence pays off. That's how it's done!" his mother said. Luke had spent the past two years at a private school that his parents couldn't really afford, and he had been miserable. But the alternative was the low-performing neighborhood high school, and Georgia and Frank wouldn't let him go there.

They started blading down the path. "It is a little intimidating, now, to be one of many artists instead of the only one."

"I can understand that."

"I'm up to the challenge, though!"

"It takes courage to live a creative life. I bet you'll make some great friends."

"Yeah, there are a lot of kids who seem cool." Friends would be nice. He had gotten a reputation as a loner at the private school, only hanging out with his girlfriend, Sarah. "I met a guy named Joaquin today. He lives up near us. I'll probably see him on the subway."

"Any cute girls?" Georgia asked.

"Mom! Okay, sure there are." There was a pit inside his stomach. Sarah, whom he had been with for two years, had moved back to England at the beginning of the summer, and he had to admit that he'd been moping around. They had decided to stay friends but not have a long-distance relationship.

"Have you heard from Sarah?"

"I see her updates on Facebook. She has a new boyfriend evidently."

"Isn't it a gorgeous day?" Georgia said. Oh good, she was changing the subject. "C'mon! Let's get up some speed!" She looked back at him and arched an eyebrow. "Maybe I should have dragged you to a yoga class. Slower pace? Get you out of your head?"

Luke smiled. She was always trying to get him out of his head. "There's no way that you could have dragged me to yoga. Blading is Zen enough."

"That's the spirit!"

Luke had been asleep by ten that night. He didn't even see Georgia the next morning. She was in the shower when he left for school, and he never saw her again.

• • •

Jim had stopped singing, pulled over the car, and put his arm around Luke's shoulders. And for some strange reason, Luke wasn't embarrassed that he was crying. It had been a relief. He hadn't felt it necessary to explain. Jim did enough talking for both of them, enough for Luke to start feeling a slim connection to another human being.

"We're a lot alike, you and me," Jim had said as Luke wiped his sleeve across his face. "I had to get away from my family too when I was your age. You know, my dad was a Baptist minister with a mean streak. And a drunk. When I met Clare, I was eighteen, and from then on, she and her mother became my family. They were my saviors."

"What happened to your parents?"

"Ah," Jim had begun, "our relationship was bad enough when I left for college, but when Clare got pregnant, they completely disowned me. It's sad, yes, but we haven't spoken all these years, and that is a story I still don't know the end to."

"Well, how did you meet Clare?"

"At the restaurant that became my life. I was a freshman at the state college, working as a waiter, and she was the hostess on the weekends. We got pregnant with Ava toward the end of Clare's senior year of high school. I quit college and worked my way up in the restaurant business. And then moving to Moab—it's given me a second chance. The last couple of years in Cleveland, with Clare's mother dying, well, I made some big mistakes, and Clare and I almost split up. But I wasn't going to let that happen. Moving here has given us the opportunity to start over, to do what we love, to be happy. We're empty nesters, after all."

"Oh yeah, your daughter, Ava."

"She's about your age and is also a lot like us. Some people need to find their own way."

Us.

"You're in the right place, Luke, it's okay."

Then Jim had given him his first driving lesson.

• • •

Luke drove the two miles to the behemoth of a supermarket. Not like the small, compact stores of New York City. Here real estate was less of an issue, so the supermarket sprawled out. Moab, the town itself, was ugly; there was no way to be nice about it. Besides the grocery eyesore, there were several fast-food chains, gas stations, tour outfits, and some boutiques and restaurants in the center. Cheesy New Age shops like Crystal Mania and Shamans-for-Hire. There were masseuses, specialists in vision quests, Native American spiritualists (as opposed to shamans), crystal healers, yogis—you name it.

The first red light on the way to the supermarket was a long one, and Luke looked over at the Dairy Queen, a popular hangout. Jen was there in short shorts and a bathing suit top, sitting with some sketchy characters on the wall next to the parking lot.

The light changed. Luke passed the bike shop and thought about making a stop to drool over the mountain bikes. He was going to buy one as soon as he had saved up enough money. He was lucky though to have use of the Bronco pretty much whenever he needed it.

Next door to the bike shop was Red Rock Rafting Tours, and he wondered how Tangerine was doing. He kept driving; he would stop by on the way back. He was glad that Cin had come over last night. Cin, like so many others here, was teaching Luke how to be devoted to the present.

• • •

Tangerine had her nose in a guidebook when Luke walked into the Red Rock building, the bell on the door jingling.

"Hey, stranger! Cin's out on a tour."

"How's it going?" he asked as he looked around at all the boating paraphernalia.

"It's really no worries. But she does need someone minding the store and taking reservations. She can't be in two places at once. She's evidently made quite a name for herself. People ask for Cin specifically to be their tour guide."

"I wonder how they know about her."

"The Web site, darling." There was her soft smile. Her exuberance left him feeling a little dizzy. He looked around some more, trying to think of something to say, or a question to ask. An excuse to stay longer.

"Um . . . how many tour guides are there?"

"Four. Have you ever been on the river?"

Luke shook his head.

"Unbelievable. You've been here for eight months and you haven't gone on it yet?"

"Well, not since I was a kid."

"Then you have to come with us tomorrow. Cin thinks that I should be familiar with the tour, so we're going to take a special trip in the morning. You have to get someone else to cover for you at the Moonflower so you can come."

"Yeah?"

"Yeah!"

"Okay."

"And tonight is supposed to be the best night for shooting stars, so we have to go to Slickrock after the barbecue. You game?"

"I'm game."

"Good. Oh, Luke, I'm so glad that I have a reason to stay! I didn't really want to leave Moab yet, and I'm certainly not ready to go back to Holy Wells. So what are *you* doing so far from home?"

"Home?"

"The Moonflower."

"Oh. I, um, got some groceries for the canteen and the barbecue."

"Are you going to make anything?"

"Clare asked me to make cowboy salad."

"What's that?"

"Oh, it's really easy. Black beans, corn, lime, cilantro, and lots of avocado."

"Yum! I'll help you if you want!"

"Okay, sure, well . . ."

Tangerine looked at her watch. "Cin will be done soon. I have to drive her Jeep to pick her up and help her de-rig . . . and then I'll be back at the Moonflower and we can hang out!"

She was making it effortless for him. "See you later then," Luke said, as the door jingled again on his way out.

four

It was almost 6:00 p.m., and Ava had been working at the Living Room Lounge for the past four hours. She knew that she was lucky to have this job, but the effects of the morning meeting were wearing off. She didn't know if she could take it anymore. Not drinking was almost impossible here. What was the point in staying sober? Maybe fifty-eight days was enough. Sobriety was excruciating on a shift like this, a busy Saturday, which was just going to get busier as the night wore on.

The Living Room Lounge was supposed to be a café, but with all the alcohol she served, it might as well be a bar.

"I'd like a beer."

"How's the Chardonnay?"

"The Merlot?"

"What's your house red like?"

How would I fucking know? she wanted to scream. What was that load of crap AA was shoving down her throat? *Don't think, don't drink, and go to meetings.* It was a cult, she knew it. They were brainwashing her. She could have a drink. One or two. Help her get through the night. Later. "Keep putting it off every five minutes," Charlie had said. "And then call me before you do it." *But then he'll talk me out of it* . . . "Do the next right thing that will lead you closer to your Higher Power and away from a drink." Yeah, it was a cult.

Ava was born to be a waitress, having grown up in the restaurant business. She could do it stoned and drunk, deaf, dumb, and blind. Just not sober. She had been working here three nights a week since last summer, when she'd seen the Help Wanted sign and walked in like she owned the place. Where had all that confidence gone?

• • •

Ava had been thrilled to get out of Ohio. She could reinvent herself in New York City. Her parents would let her do just about anything because she had gotten into Barnard, and Nana had left her the money to pay for college.

The drive east had been tedious, Jim and Clare barely speaking to each other in the front as Ava stared out the window, fantasizing about life in New York City. She had found a small studio sublet on 106th Street, near Barnard, on Craigslist. The dorms were too expensive, and she wanted to get a job and prove that she could do everything on her own.

She would be eighteen in November.

"Are you sure you don't need any money?" Jim had asked.

"You don't have to support me anymore, Jim. I'll get a job in a restaurant."

"What happened to calling us Mom and Dad?" Clare had asked.

"It's fine. Call me whatever you want, honey," Jim had said.

They'd unpacked the car: a futon, bedding, and a few suitcases.

"Shouldn't we stay, and help you get settled?" Clare had asked.

"I'm great. You guys go off on your road trip, and I'll see you Labor Day weekend, before school starts, okay?"

"We are so proud of you," Clare had told her.

"Yeah, thanks."

And they'd driven off.

Ava, armed with her fake ID, had walked around the neighborhood and started barhopping.

· · ·

An hour later, and Ava's mood still hadn't improved. She didn't see how she would make it until midnight without doing something crazy, and she was too stubborn to call Charlie. This was supposed to be an easy job, a no-brainer. But her feelings were intense, everything was too 3-D, larger than life, louder than life. It was all so tempting.

Okay, five minutes, let me get through the next five minutes.

"Um, can you ask him to salt the margarita glass, miss?"

Ava found herself nodding and collecting more drink orders. Then she was back at the bar, and as she watched Sammy make the drinks, she could feel herself salivating.

Sammy looked at her. "You thirsty?"

"Like you wouldn't believe."

"Vodka and cranberry? Or are you still not drinking?"

Ava's heart was beating fast. "Yes." Did she just say yes to a drink? *Yes! Yes! Yes!*

"You helping me close at midnight?" Sammy asked, and Ava nodded mechanically. Sammy knew the answer to that. What game was he playing? She had arranged ten-hour shifts so that she only had to work three days a week. Sammy finished making the drinks and put them on her tray. Thank God she had never slept with him, although he tried every month or so. How had she stayed sober this long?

"I'll be right back." Ava delivered the wine, the beer, the margarita, thinking about vodka and cranberry, and the last time she had had that cocktail. She had gone to a bar called the Last Exit,

49

ostensibly just for one drink, and had ended up having God knows how many nasty concoctions and having sex with the bartender in the basement. Maybe that's why she was trying to stay sober. She couldn't live with herself, watching her actions not match who she wanted to be.

"I'll just have a cup of coffee, thanks," the woman at the corner table said. Huh? She couldn't account for the last minute or so.

"Got it." She turned around and went behind the bar to the coffee machine. Sammy grazed her breast with his meaty hand as he put a red drink in front of her. She froze with revulsion for Sammy and desire for the drink.

"What are you doing after we close?" Eew. Gross. But then again, she was gross. But then again, she didn't have to put up with that. And she didn't have to drink. She rolled her eyes at Sammy. What was she doing? Getting coffee. The drink would still be there. She poured the coffee and took the cup over to the woman at the table.

"Here you go," she said, and put it down.

Ava took a deep breath. She could do it. She went back to the bar.

"Hey, Sam-I-am." She picked up her drink and toasted Sammy, then poured it down the sink.

"Geez, Ave."

"I need a break."

Sammy nodded, looking a little flushed himself. Why he hadn't fired her ass yet was beyond her.

• • •

Fresh air. Not so fresh air, August in New York, but she needed to walk in a straight line to escape the chaos. Literally. She started walking up Amsterdam Avenue from 107th Street. The café had been crowded, but the streets were empty. Morningside Heights in

August was deadville. The sun was glistening off the windows of the tall buildings engulfing her, buildings that gave not only the streets but herself a kind of structure. She was in a man-made canyon, and if she wasn't so mad, it would have been beautiful. She was capable of finding beauty in the world sometimes. She had to remember that. What had just happened? She hadn't drunk. Then why was she angry?

She tried to remember the other night with Charlie, when they had taken the Big Book and some sandwiches on the Staten Island Ferry.

"Just for the ride," Charlie had said.

•   •   •

They stood in the front of the ferry and talked, the breezes off New York Harbor washing over them.

"How do you do it?" Ava asked. "How do you stay sober and happy? How do you know what to do?"

"It's very simple, sweets," Charlie said. "Baby steps. Do whatever is in front of you that will lead you closer to your Higher Power."

Ava shook her head. "I'm not getting all of this 'Higher Power' stuff yet. Break it down for me."

"Okay. Just do the next right thing."

"That's it?"

"That's it."

Ava thought about that. "But how do I know what the next right thing is?"

"Now that takes practice, but I can help you. Not into prayer? Seek silence, calm the emotions, say a mantra. Call me!"

"Oh, Charlie." Ava felt her nose tingle and her eyes smart. "Why are you helping me?"

He laughed. "It's purely selfish. It helps me stay sober, helping you. And, I happen to like you and relate to you. Can't find better reasons than that."

"Am I ever going to have fun again?"

"Yes—but your definition of fun will change. You will learn how to have joy in your life, I promise—as long as you do exactly what I tell you to do." She gave him a baffled look. "I'm joking." But jokes always had some truth to them. "Yes, I have a tendency to overdo it. I always seem to know what other people should do. There have only been a couple of times when I was baffled about what the next right thing was . . . for somebody else. It drives my boyfriend, Alec, crazy. The hardest thing for me to do is keep the focus on myself, instead of saving everybody else."

They had to get off the ferry and then get on a different one to head back to the city. "You should have been a nurse," Ava said dryly as they boarded the Manhattan-bound ferry.

"Do I remind you of your mother? I get that all the time. Let's go up to the front, so we can see the lights." It wasn't crowded, because it was ten o'clock at night. The ferry started to move.

"Start spreading the news . . ." *Oh, God.* Charlie was singing. "I'm leaving today . . ."

She found herself joining in despite herself. "I want to be a part of it, New York, New York . . ."

"These vagabond shoes . . ." All of a sudden, she was having fun. She was singing with another human being, and she was having fun. She was part of the human race. She lost all self-consciousness as they sang song after song, making up the words they didn't know and watching the city rise before them.

• • •

Ava knew she had to quit serving drinks, she obviously couldn't be around alcohol. That was the next right thing. But she needed the money! Maybe she could get someone from AA to sit in the café every night. She needed a sitter. *I need a freaking babysitter?* Why was everything so hard? She wished she could be little again, and crawl into Nana's lap, and have Nana lie and say that everything was going to be just dandy and work out fine.

She wanted a mother. She *had* a mother, but how could she tell her that she was an alcoholic, that she wasn't the strong person Clare thought she was? Forget about Jim for the moment. They had both left her so many messages, but she couldn't bear to hear their voices and pressed Delete right away. She couldn't bear to be reminded that she wasn't the person they thought she was, who she wanted to be. Great. Underneath all that anger was a big ball of fear.

five

Luke had some time to kill before he had to get ready for the barbe-cue, so he tried to take a nap, but he couldn't find a comfortable position. Sleep was hard enough in the heat, but he hadn't noticed while he was working how much his body hurt. He must have pulled something scrambling down from Angel Rock.

He wanted to think about Tangerine, but his thoughts brought him back to the weirdness of last night. Who could he tell? Not Tangerine, she'd think he was a freak. He could confide in Jim, but maybe this was too much. Cin would be the obvious person to talk to about animal visions, but frankly, he thought, it would be better to forget about it, the way he was trying to erase all of the other things that disturbed him.

• • •

It had been a Thursday in December, a week before the school holi-day break, and Luke had borrowed Frank's Columbia alumnus ID and hung out in Butler Library all day. At the beginning of the month, Frank's bereavement leave of absence from his job teaching English at the middle school had become permanent. If Frank wasn't going back to work, Luke thought he might as well stop going to school. He came home to a pile of dishes in the kitchen sink, garbage strewn across the floor, and Frank passed out on Luke's bed. The door to Frank's room was closed. Luke pushed it open partway and staggered back, the stench overwhelming him. Frank had vomited in his bed and, instead of cleaning it up, had fallen asleep in Luke's bed.

It might have been okay if this was the first time it had happened. It might have been okay if Frank had the stomach flu. But it wasn't, and he didn't.

"Jesus Christ, Frank." Luke slammed his father's bedroom door shut, shaking with anger.

Charlie had told him that the definition of insanity was doing the same thing over and over again and expecting different results. Well, then, Frank was definitely insane, and Luke might as well be too.

The apartment used to seem big to Luke, when it was the three of them. It was a rent-stabilized two-bedroom in a prewar Columbia building on 121st Street and Amsterdam Avenue that Frank had been grandfathered into during his Teachers College days. It was cluttered but well put together. It looked like a library, with floor-to-ceiling bookshelves in the living room and the bedrooms. But now that it was just the two of them, it felt claustrophobic. The clutter was just clutter.

Luke had gone back to school a few days after Georgia's death, walking the halls in a daze. Nobody knew him, so he didn't have to tell anyone anything. But he couldn't paint. He distanced himself from his old friends, who didn't know what to say anyway. He certainly never e-mailed Sarah.

The day Georgia died, she had taken a taxi to work. Luke could imagine her, anxiously looking at her watch at 8:25 a.m., worried that she would be late for her 8:30 client. The taxi ran through a yellow light as an SUV swung around the corner and pushed them onto the sidewalk, injuring a pedestrian. Georgia must not have been wearing a seat belt because she somersaulted into the front seat, her neck snapping back, DOA. It could have happened to anyone.

But it happened to Georgia, to him, to Frank. Frank had his first drink that night, and Luke went on automatic pilot. He avoided Frank and home as much as possible. He attended just enough school so that he wouldn't attract negative attention and spent most of his time walking around the city or at Butler Library, reading and pretending to be someone else. He would come home periodically and have to clean and take out Frank's empty bottles. Luke had his own bank account, but they weren't going to survive off of that. He found his parents' bank statements and the checkbook, paid the rent on time, and bought groceries. Georgia and Frank had both taken out pretty generous life insurance policies, so they would be all right for a couple of years if Frank couldn't get his act together.

It didn't take long for Charlie to stage a series of interventions, but nobody could get sober for Frank. Even Luke knew that. Frank was killing himself. Luke had never known that loneliness could be so horrible. He knew that Frank had loved him and he had loved Frank before Georgia died, but those memories were being slowly erased by Frank's drinking.

Frank moaned from behind the door.

"Frank?" Luke opened it again. "Frank, will you let me take you to the hospital?"

His father moaned again and then opened his eyes and stared at Luke.

"Leave me alone."

I can't live here anymore. I can't live this way. But where can I go? Frank's parents were dead, and he had been estranged from the rest of his family for as long as Luke could remember. Frank always said that AA was his family. Georgia had been an only child, and her mother was living in a retirement village in Florida. They were not close.

Charlie. He'd go to Charlie and figure it out from there.

"Frank." No answer. He couldn't deal with cleaning up Frank's mess. Even one more time.

Luke stuffed some clothes in a backpack and walked the few blocks to Charlie's apartment on 114th Street. It was a frigid December day, dark already. He could see his breath as he walked down the hill from Amsterdam to Broadway. Charlie had been in their lives since Luke was six and Frank had sponsored him. Charlie became family. Charlie made Luke feel respected and valued. Why couldn't Frank be like that anymore? Why couldn't he stop drinking?

Luke walked up the steps to Charlie's building and pressed 3D, but there was no answer. He waited. He had nothing else to do, nowhere else to go.

The idea of leaving, not just leaving Frank but leaving New York altogether, started to germinate in Luke's head right there.

Charlie had done everything he could, taking him out for pizza, to meetings of Al-Anon—a twelve-step program for families of alcoholics. *I am powerless over Frank's alcoholism . . . well, duh.* But he didn't want "support," he wanted the impossible. He wanted the world to go back to the way it was before.

Luke shivered in his bomber jacket. He felt pathetic, and he didn't want to feel pathetic anymore. He was going to leave. He would figure things out for himself. He made up his mind. For the first time in months, he started to feel a glimmer of hope. He finally saw Charlie walking down the street, holding hands with Alec. Charlie waved.

"Luke, what are you doing here?" he asked. They walked up the steps, and Charlie put his hand on Luke's shoulder while Alec opened the door to the building. "How long have you been waiting?"

"Listen, Charlie, I've had enough. I've got to get out of there. I can't take it anymore."

"I know, Luke. Come inside and we'll talk about it. I'm so sorry that you have to go through this. It's hard enough for me to watch, but you—"

Luke shrugged his shoulders, following them into the building.

"Of course you inherited an unearthly stoicism from your beautiful mother. Any ideas? What's your next right thing?" This was Charlie's favorite advice, advice that he had gotten from Frank years ago: *Do the next right thing . . .*

Luke was quiet as they climbed the stairs to the third floor. He hadn't known until then, but he saw, with perfect clarity, where he wanted to go, what his next right thing was. Alec held open the door to their apartment and then went into the kitchen, leaving them alone.

"I want to leave. I want to go to Moab," Luke said.

"Do what?"

"I'm going to move to Moab."

"You can't." Charlie looked alarmed. "That's not the next right thing. That's called running away."

"How do you know what my next right thing is?"

"Luke, you're sixteen. You've lost your mother and you're losing your father."

"Well, when you put it like that . . ."

"You need someone to take care of you."

"And who is going to do that? I've been trying to take care of both of us for over three months! In those Al-Anon meetings you made me go to, they say I can't change Frank, I can only change myself."

"Yes, we can only change ourselves, but—moving across the country? At sixteen? I understand that you think you know Moab, that it's familiar, but you haven't been there in years."

"Four years ago we camped in the canyonlands for two weeks. I know how to do that."

58

"Luke, this isn't the Boy Scouts. You think you can leave your life behind to go camping in Utah? I can't let you do something this extreme. Let's think of other options, options for you in New York. Finishing high school isn't a bad idea. You worked so hard at getting into art school."

Luke watched Charlie put away his coat and gloves. "I know. It's pathetic, isn't it? I can't paint anymore anyway."

Charlie looked at Luke for a long time. "Let's concentrate on getting Frank into rehab."

"We've tried! He won't go. I'm telling you, Charlie, he's gone. I should take you over to the apartment right now. You wouldn't believe the state it's in."

"Okay. Well, so we'll get you out of there . . . What about your grandmother?"

"Come on. You mean go to Florida? No. She can barely take care of herself."

"Right . . ."

"What about you?" Luke played his trump card. He knew perfectly well what the answer would be. Charlie lived in a studio, and Alec had just moved in with him. But Charlie looked like he was considering it.

"What are you telling the school about your situation?"

"I am barely at school. And if I told anybody what was really going on, they would run to Social Services and I'd go to foster care or a group home. Don't make me do that."

"Okay. Stay with us for now, and we'll try to help Frank together. Then we'll figure something out for you."

• • •

Luke lay on the bed in the trailer, hands clasped beneath his head. He couldn't think about Frank anymore. He knew from occasional phone calls with Charlie that nothing had changed—Frank was still drinking.

He sat up and stretched his arms over his head. His temples throbbed. His stomach grumbled, and he was actually grateful for that distraction. Grateful for thoughts of barbecued ribs and cowboy salad, much better than these other thoughts.

• • •

Clare was behind the front desk when Luke walked in.

"Hey," Luke said. She was on the phone and held up a finger. He went into the common room. Bruno was by himself, watching *Meerkat Manor* on Animal Planet with the sound off.

"What's up?" Luke said as he sat down on a couch.

"Hey, man." Bruno looked furtively around. "I'm avoiding Dom."

"She checked out already."

"Really?" Was that disappointment on Bruno's face? "She wasn't here long. Come to think of it, I'm the one who's been coasting here too long." Bruno sighed. His eyes returned to the meerkats, and Luke relaxed more into the couch, mesmerized by them himself until Tangerine's voice broke him out of his reverie.

"Happy birthday!" he heard her say from the other room. Whose birthday was it?

"Oh, thank you!" It was Clare's. "How did she do on her first day at Red Rock?" Cin must have come in with Tangerine.

"She's single-handedly saving the reputation of Red Rock Rafting Tours!" Cin said.

"Yeah, right." Luke could almost see Tangerine's nose crinkle. "So, Clare, it's your birthday. How do you feel?"

"Great, for the most part. This year has been a good one. I've written a ton of poetry! It was right to move here, to change paths.

I was so burnt out on nursing, the hospital and the bureaucracy. I just miss Ava."

"When is she going to come visit?" Tangerine asked.

Clare sighed. "She's angry at us. She didn't want us to move. She just seems to get angrier—she hasn't been in touch for two months. I'm holding out hope that she'll call me today, for my birthday. I see what you are thinking, you two, and I do call her, but she's left an outgoing message on her cell phone that says something like 'I'm okay, Mom, I just can't talk to you right now.'"

"It must worry you," Tangerine said. "My mum would die if I didn't call her every week."

"Of course! But Jim thinks that she's just asserting her individuality. And I leave messages for her. I don't know what else there is to do, short of flying out there and banging on her door. Maybe I should." The phone rang again. "Would you answer that and watch the desk for a while, Tangerine? I have to go upstairs."

"Moonflower Motel, may I help you?"

There was something off about what Clare had said. Luke had been a little envious of the unknown Ava, the lucky girl who had parents like Jim and Clare. Now the picture of them as a happy family started to fray around the edges.

He pushed himself out of the couch, stood up, and stretched. He went into the other room and caught a glimpse of Cin as she followed Clare into the part of the Moonflower that was her home. Tangerine was still on the phone, so he walked back to the kitchen and started rummaging around for a can opener.

"I thought I heard you," Tangerine said after she hung up. "What can I do to help you with your salad?"

"Want to take the corn out of the freezer and nuke it in the microwave?" he asked.

Tangerine opened the freezer. "Both of them?"

"Sure." He found a colander, put it in the sink, and emptied five cans of black beans into it.

"Where'd you learn to cook?"

"My mom. We used to take turns making dinner for each other. My dad wasn't usually around at dinnertime." That was all he wanted to say about Frank. An image of the "after" Frank popped into his mind: dirty, smelly, skinny, godless, a terrified creature. The "before" Frank was charismatic, bright, kind, but he put his sobriety before everything, eschewing dinner with his family for meetings, always doing "service," helping others in recovery. How could Frank have been so certain, and then given all that up?

Ask *her* a question. "How about you?"

"I dunno, really. We all had to take turns too. Turns doing everything. There are nine of us! Two parents and seven kids." She sounded wistful.

"You must miss them then."

"Of course! Don't you?" Luke couldn't have looked more awkward. "I mean, oh gosh, foot in my mouth, I remember now . . . But what about your dad? Oh, there I go again, you don't have to answer. I just want to know everything about everyone, but I don't have to." The microwave beeped, and Tangerine took the corn out. "Shall we mix this together, then?"

Luke nodded, relieved that they had a task to focus on. He sliced open a lime and squeezed the juice onto the beans and corn.

"Would you rather chop onion or cilantro?" he asked Tangerine.

"Both!" She found a knife and cutting board to work with.

"Um, Tangerine—what is it like being the only sister with six brothers?"

She laughed. "I get asked that *a lot*! Believe me, it's hard to do anything with them around! Nobody wants that kind of scrutiny. So when I turned eighteen, my parents cut me loose. I went to Bali with a girlfriend for a couple of months, but I thought I really needed to be on my own, to find out who I am and make my own decisions. So I came to America."

"Well, you're doing a good job, on your own."

"And I'm staying! I'll go back though . . . In a few months, if I get more work after August. Do you want help with those avocados?"

"Sure. We need more lime juice too."

• • •

Luke devoured Clare's spareribs. Tangerine was sitting very close, but she was turned away from him, listening to Brigitte tell a story about grad school. She had brought Carlos, a nice guy who worked for the Moab to Monument Valley Film Commission. It was a beautiful evening, and a slight breeze tinged the air with sage and, well, yes, meat. Luke could feel himself beginning to relax. He looked over at Bruno, who raised a rib in salute and kept eating. There were more than the usual cast of characters here—all the Moonflower guests were present, including Magda, who was the oldest person he had ever seen staying at the Moonflower. "Youth isn't only for the young," she had said when she checked in that morning. Jim and Clare had invited some of the locals as well, to help celebrate Clare's birthday. But the locals were only as "local" as he was. There was Cin, of course; and Chavez, a hairdresser originally from Santa Fe; Cha'tima, Jim's friend who had grown up on the Hopi reservation in northeastern Arizona; Carson, a former airline pilot who did helicopter tours in the area; Susan and Maureen, a couple from Portland who now owned the organic market; Oswald, the police chief, who was a native; and the

Fiddlers Three as they called themselves, even though there were only two now: Paul, a teacher at the local high school, and Melinda, a therapist at the mental health center. They were lamenting that the third fiddler had just moved back to Chicago.

Luke watched Jim grilling and laughing at something Clare was saying. He could see how much they loved each other and felt a warm pang, both joy and sadness. He couldn't believe how hungry he was; he felt like a bottomless pit. He poured himself a glass of lemonade.

"Some appetite!"

Luke smiled sheepishly and looked up at Carson, who had spotted the bones on his plate.

"Yeah, Clare is an amazing cook," Luke said.

"I heard that, Luke. I'll have you know that the barbecue sauce is *my* secret recipe," Jim said.

"It's true, sometimes I just feel like the sous chef, doing all of the grunt work," Clare said, laughing. "But, Luke, your cowboy salad is the hit of the party." She lifted up the bowl and showed him that it was empty. Luke gave her a thumbs-up.

Carson intrigued Luke—he'd never actually met a pilot before. He wanted to go for a ride in Carson's helicopter and could imagine that seeing the canyons and the arches from the sky was incredible. He tuned in to the conversation at the table, Susan telling some others about a drumming circle that they were going to later. Luke shook his head absentmindedly.

"Not a fan of drumming circles, I take it?" Carson sat down across from him.

Luke laughed. "Nah. It's just a big excuse to smoke dope, and make people think they've seen spirits."

Tangerine turned toward him, words almost on her lips, but

Clare started clapping and saying, "Paul, Melinda, play for us! Sing for your supper!" Luke wondered what Tangerine had been about to say. Paul grinned while Melinda looked shy, but they lovingly picked up their violins and started playing very fast, very lively.

Luke heard the ringing of Clare's cell phone. She answered and listened, a frown on her face. "Hold on a minute, stop yelling!" Clare was speaking so forcefully into the phone that the musicians stopped playing. "I haven't seen her. She's not here." Pause. "I'm worried too. I'll call you if I hear anything." Clare hung up the phone. "Has anybody seen Jen? She's missing. Bill's insisting that she's here, Jim."

"It's okay, Clare." Jim put his arm around her.

"Well, Bill sounded more mad at me than anything else. He practically accused me of stealing his daughter."

"Has she run away again?" Tangerine asked.

"I'd shoot myself if she was my daughter," Paul said.

"I saw her earlier today in front of the Dairy Queen," Luke offered. "She was sitting with a couple of guys."

"Sometimes this place feels like a halfway house." Clare said. *Ouch.* "Oh. She said that she had met a guy—Jaime, new in town. Does anybody know who he is?"

"I hope it's not who I think it is," Oswald said. "A few weeks ago I arrested a guy named Jaime from Arizona for possession of crystal meth. But his parents are bigwigs from Tucson, flew in and posted bail . . . so I had to let him go."

"Sounds like it could be the same guy." Clare turned toward Jim. "But Jen said that he was staying with his parents at one of the campgrounds on Kane Creek Road. Do we pass this information on to Bill and Kerri or investigate ourselves?"

Oswald shook his head. "I'll handle it. Sounds like you're already caught in the middle, and this isn't your problem to solve."

"But you're off duty," Clare said.

"Not anymore. Besides, Bill and I went to high school together. I'll go on over and talk to him, and then I'll see if I can find Jaime. Probably there's nothing to worry about."

"Oh, I think there is plenty to worry about if she's been hanging out with a guy who has easy access to drugs and parents who throw money at problems," Jim said.

"We don't know for sure that it's the same guy," Clare said.

Luke thought about Frank. Instead of being a "problem" child, he had a "problem" parent, a "problem" he couldn't solve.

• • •

Luke had stayed that week before Christmas with Charlie and Alec, sleeping on the sofa. He tried to stay out of their way as much as possible, but he could tell that he was cramping their style and that Alec was becoming resentful. Charlie went to check on Frank every day, but Frank "didn't want Charlie's pity or charity."

They talked over and over again about what Luke should do, but Luke knew what he wanted. He imagined that he could take a bus all the way to Moab. He was sure he could find a job. He could take care of himself much better there, in a small tourist town, far away from Frank, than he could in the city.

On Christmas Eve, they ordered Chinese takeout. "I'm leaving tomorrow," Luke said as he bit into an egg roll. The trip would be his Christmas present to himself.

Charlie sighed. "I guess you are. I don't know what to do about Frank anymore either. Can you remember him being a good dad? Can you see that he's a sick man and that this is a disease?"

Luke couldn't answer that directly. "I guess you could say that I don't want to be a third casualty."

"The condition is"—Charlie waved a forkful of noodles at him—"the condition is that you have to go say goodbye. Now that is as much for you as it is for him. Maybe we'll have a miracle and he'll snap out of it."

Luke grinned. "I have to get my things anyway."

"Why don't we go up there after we eat? See if we can shake some sense into him."

They walked up Broadway from 114th to 121st Street and rode the elevator to the fifth floor in silence. Luke unlocked the door, and the room was so quiet, it was deafening. Charlie gently pushed past him.

"Why don't you make a pot of coffee and I'll poke my head in?" Charlie said. This was his show. Luke looked around the apartment as if he were a stranger. He knew that Frank wouldn't want coffee, but he decided to make it anyway, straining to hear the murmurs in the bedroom: "Luke has come to say goodbye. He's going to Moab, unless you are willing to get some help." The coffee started to drip, and Luke walked over to the doorway.

"No." Frank's eyes were on fire. "No, I can't. I can't stop drinking. I don't want to stop drinking, I don't want to go to a meeting. I can't—" He caught sight of Luke and started to cry. "Luke, I'm sorry, sorry, sorry, sorry. So sorry."

"If you're sorry, do something about it. Go back to AA." Luke said the words, but his heart wasn't in it.

"AA? AA is crap. The twelve steps are crap. There is no Higher Power."

Luke felt anger shoot up into his heart and out his throat. "Okay, kill yourself then." He wanted to punch his father, to kick his head in, to finish the job, but he walked into the living room instead. "Goodbye."

He heard Charlie say, "You have something to stay sober for.

You have Luke. You have yourself. You have a life that's worth living already. But alcohol is robbing you of that."

"I don't care anymore." Magic words. Charlie threw his hands up in exasperation and backed out of the bedroom, closing the door. Luke stood motionless in the middle of the living room. He could hear his heart pounding and feel his fists itching.

Charlie stared at him for a long time before saying, "He doesn't mean it, Luke. That was the booze talking, not your dad."

Luke nodded, but he was upset. His rage surprised him, because he had what he'd thought he wanted. Nothing was standing in the way of his leaving. "Was that enough of a goodbye?" he asked. He went to the closet and pulled the small tent out. He grabbed his sleeping bag and an empty duffel, dislodging some smaller boxes, which fell on top of him. He yelled in frustration as Charlie rushed to help him put the boxes back. Luke went to his room and stuffed clothes haphazardly into his bag. He glanced at his portfolio and considered taking it but then decided against it. Art was part of his past. Charlie was still in the living room as Luke bulldozed in with his stuff. His eyes rested on the painting. Georgia's painting. His painting. *Fuck you, Dad. You can't have it.* He dropped his bags on the floor and lifted the painting off the hook.

"You're taking that?" Charlie asked.

Luke nodded.

"What's your money situation?"

Luke had already thought that through. "I'll explain once we get out of here." He went to the desk in the corner and grabbed the checkbook. "Let's go."

As they walked the few blocks downtown, Luke said, "I have about fifteen hundred dollars in my own bank account. I know that's not a lot of money, but if I'm frugal I can make it stretch until I find a job. I've been paying the rent and the bills and whatnot for

Frank by forging his signature. I'm going to write a check to cover all of next year . . . He'll get evicted if the rent isn't paid. If I could leave some blank checks here for you to pay the other bills, that would be great."

"I don't know what to say. Alec thinks it's okay to let you go, that you're more mature than many of our friends who are twenty years older than you. Of course I'll take care of Frank. He took care of me. I can't give up on him." They stopped on a corner. "That came out wrong. Okay. You need to promise that we'll keep in touch. And if you want to come home, I'll send you a plane ticket, no questions asked." They crossed the street. "Here's the clincher: if Frank sobers up, we're coming to get you. I honestly don't know what the right thing is . . . I know that the easiest thing is to let you do what you want, but that's what makes me think it's not right."

Luke waited for Charlie to say more. What was his point? But when Charlie didn't continue, Luke said, "I know exactly where I'm going. I can take the bus all the way. There's a youth hostel I found on the Internet when I Googled Moab, called the Moon-flower Motel, really cheap. I'll stay there while I figure things out."

"Good. I feel better already knowing where you'll be."

They walked into Charlie's building. "Why don't we call it a night," Charlie said in the elevator, "and then tomorrow we'll have a great send-off."

• • •

The next morning they listened to Nat King Cole and drank strong coffee. While Alec was in the shower, Charlie went to the computer and printed something out.

"Merry Christmas," he said, giving Luke the piece of paper. It was a first-class train ticket to Grand Junction, Colorado.

"Oh, man, thank you."

"The bus would take forever. See, it's two trains. The first, to Chicago, takes nineteen hours. Then you have a four-hour layover, and Chicago to Grand Junction takes twenty-seven hours. Then it's a two-hour bus ride to Moab."

"But my own cabin? That's so extravagant."

"I just don't want you to be a target." Charlie made Luke promise that he would keep the door locked. Luke waited for Charlie to tell him not to talk to strangers, but even Charlie didn't go that far.

Charlie took Luke down to Penn Station on Christmas afternoon and put him on the train. It left at 3:45 p.m. Luke was in Moab two days later.

six

Ava had walked all the way up Amsterdam to 145th street, almost forty blocks, which was a couple of miles. Her cell phone had buzzed quite a few times, but she hadn't even checked: she knew it was Sammy, freaking out. Those people in the AA meetings had abused alcohol far worse than she had. She could drink for a few more years, couldn't she? When had alcohol stopped being her friend? There were so many awful things she hadn't done yet. *I haven't lost a job yet, I haven't gone to jail yet, I haven't been homeless yet.* These were all things that could happen if she didn't stay sober. *I haven't killed myself yet.* But the negative thoughts, the self-hatred had brought her to the edge of suicide too many times.

She could almost taste the vodka she had poured down the sink, and she shuddered.

Her feet turned around and started walking back downtown. It was eight o'clock already, and she had taken a very long break. She groaned and pulled out her cell phone. She had never been this irresponsible on the job. Sammy had left four messages. *Why not quit? Why not trust that the farther away I am from booze, the saner I'll feel? Why not trust that I can find another job?* Where were these thoughts coming from? There was a precision and clarity to them, stronger than the voice saying *I want to drink.* She was going to return to the Living

Room Lounge and quit. She'd figure out what to do about a new job later. She was bound to drink if she kept working there. If not tonight, then some other night.

The air was sticky, and salsa music blared from a car radio. Ava was lost in her thoughts so much of the time that she barely noticed her surroundings, getting closer and closer to the café as the blue of the sky darkened and the streetlamps turned on, promising the evening. She walked past the Italian building at Columbia and the School of International Affairs. Across the street from St. Luke's Hospital, Ava saw a guy holding on to a lamppost. Hugging the lamppost? As she walked closer, she felt a shock of recognition. Al Pacino? It was Charlie's friend from the meeting. He looked grotesque under the glow of the streetlight, like some wraith, a phantom. Death. Waiting. For . . . *it isn't me, it isn't me, it isn't me . . .*

"Hey. Are you okay?" Recognition registered on Frank's face as he turned his head toward her voice. She looked down and saw a puddle under his feet. He looked too and started laughing.

He said, "'To be or not to be, that is the question.'"

"Uh, yeah, my thoughts exactly." He was wasted. Why was she still standing there? "What's going on? It's none of my business, but, uh, are you drunk?"

"I wish to God I was. If I can piss myself sober, I may as well piss myself drunk."

Ava thought about that. He had a point. He was looking across the street at the hospital.

"Going over there?"

"I was, I was dragging myself there. You were at the meeting this morning?" Frank asked, and she nodded. "Charlie took me home in a cab after that, and he stayed for a while. But I've just been feeling worse and worse. I don't live far, so I thought that I could walk . . . but now I can't make up my mind."

"How about a meeting instead?"

"If there was one across the street . . . I should just go across the street to the hospital." He said this more to himself than to her. "I'm sure I have some kind of alcohol poisoning." He smiled weakly. "Liver damage. My stomach is killing me. I can't stop shaking. I'm afraid to sleep because of the nightmares. I can't stand up. I can't stay sober." Was this what alcohol poisoning looked like? His skin looked more than a little yellow. *Do I walk away? Do I help?* She looked at Frank. What did he weigh? Couldn't be more than 150 pounds. Skin and bones. She could carry him across the street.

He looked like someone this shouldn't have happened to. It shouldn't happen to anyone. Frank was scratching and twitching. He needed help. *Do the next right thing.* It would keep her from drinking for now—it would keep him from drinking too.

"C'mon." She put an arm around Frank's shoulder, smelling urine and coffee. As they waited for the light to change, Frank shook so much she could barely hold him up. They crossed the street and followed the signs to the emergency room. *What am I doing? Am I out of my mind?* Ava ignored her thoughts and led Frank through the doors, into the packed waiting room.

"Do you want me to call Charlie?" *I can't stay in here—this is as much as I can do.* "I'm going to call Charlie." She took her cell phone out of her bag and pressed the number she had designated for him. Number 2. Somebody she had been calling for only a month was number 2. Come on, Charlie. Soon his canned voice was in her ear, and after the beep she left her message: Get your butt over to the ER at St. Luke's. Your buddy Frank is in bad shape.

When she turned around, she saw that Frank had gone up to the man in the booth and was doing the first part of checking himself in. Good, he wasn't totally helpless.

seven

Luke looked at the clock. It was almost eleven. He and Cin were in the kitchen finishing up the dishes from the barbecue. Jim and Clare were trying to talk softly by the foot of the stairs. They were very somber.

"I'm really worried about Ava," Luke heard Clare say. "How can you not be?"

"She'll be taken care of," Jim said.

"By who?"

"God." Jim's simple answer.

"God will do what? Make sure she calls her parents? Pays her bills? Goes to school? Do *our* job?" Luke couldn't believe that Jim would say something so stupid. Evidently Clare couldn't either, because she stomped up the stairs yelling, "Yeah, God is really taking care of Jen. He *must* be taking care of Ava too." Jim followed her.

"Did you hear that?" Luke asked Cin, who turned off the water.

"Nope. Didn't want to. I've heard the argument before. About Ava, right? All of that spiritual stuff is semantics; I wish Clare would realize that."

"But if she cared, Clare would go see Ava in New York."

Cin studied Luke. "Yes, we could look at it that way. It really bothers you, huh?"

Luke shrugged.

"Jim thinks that the right thing to do is to allow Ava her independence and let her come around by herself. They've always treated her as if she were an equal. Clare is more ambivalent." Cin's eyes were so intense. "They're not perfect, but it doesn't mean that they're not good people." She surveyed the kitchen. "Okay, great. Everything looks done here."

Luke walked into the common room, where Tangerine was playing cards with Magda.

"Gin. Again."

"Magda, you are on fire." Tangerine turned to Luke and Cin. "She's beaten me twice."

"Well, I've had a lot more practice than you." Magda had a warm smile, and her eyes twinkled mischievously.

"You're awesome."

"What, an old biddy like me?"

"Yeah, well, most old people don't go traveling by themselves and staying in youth hostels. And your schedule!"

"Yup. Whirlwind tour I'm doing. Two nights in each place I go, while my eyesight is still good enough to drive."

"Want to play a round with us, Luke?" Tangerine asked.

Luke grabbed a chair and sat down while Magda shuffled.

"I asked her to come with us tomorrow morning, Cin. She's never been rafting."

"You're in for a treat. We're doing a nice, gentle ride," Cin said. "I've got to go, so I'll see you at ten. Oh, better make that nine-thirty," she instructed, and she left.

Magda looked after her. "To tell you the truth, I almost went on one of those cruises. But I said to myself, Self, your husband is dead and gone, you would just feel lonely and crazy. Besides, if I did this very same thing by myself fifty years ago, touring the country and staying in youth hostels, why can't I do it now?"

Magda dealt them seven cards each. She looked at her hand and cackled. Tangerine put her hand over her eyes and groaned.

Luke absentmindedly played the game, thinking about the conversation he had overheard. He knew that Jim believed in God, but what kind of God? God didn't necessarily take care of anyone. Life was random, chaotic.

Replace "God" with "Higher Power," and Jim sounded like Frank. Frank always used to say that crap, whenever Luke had a problem: "Your Higher Power will take care of you." He said it so much that, eventually, Luke stopped telling his father anything. Anyway, it turned out not to be true. Was Georgia's taxi ride part of the grand plan for their family?

Okay, maybe Jim's God didn't meddle. Maybe he believed that everyone had their own private God. Georgia had believed that God was a part of her, a part of everything. That was a little better, but it still didn't make any sense to him. People's beliefs were their reality; thus they were real. Then it made sense that Jim would leave Ava to her own devices. Lucky for him, in the world according to Jim, he didn't even have to lie, he could just *be*.

• • •

"The stars aren't moving, but they're spectacular," Tangerine said. They were lying back on the hood of the Bronco, having driven up to Slickrock.

"Haven't you ever seen a shooting star?" Luke said. "There must be big open sky in Holy Wells. Look—there's one!"

"Where? Oh, darnit. Sure, I've seen them before. I guess I'm just having a hard time focusing tonight. I keep trying to see the bears."

"There are bears in the sky?" Luke asked.

"Yeah, the Big Dipper is part of the constellation Ursa Major, and the Little Dipper is part of Ursa Minor, the Great and Little Bears."

How could I have forgotten that?

"I can see the dippers, just not the bears. Oh! There's one!" Tangerine said.

"A bear or a shooting star?"

"And another one! I'm seeing them now."

"Yeah, the trick is to just look at one patch of the sky."

He looked at the Big Dipper too. Where was the bear? Shooting stars were unbelievable. He'd never seen so many.

Luke could feel that some strands of Tangerine's hair had landed on his shoulder. The silence between them felt electric. He wanted to hold her hand. Should he?

"'God's in his heaven—all's right with the world,'" Tangerine said.

"Huh?"

"This is where I feel God. Nature, the elements. Not church. My family is super Christian—Jesus is the only way. That can't be true, can it?"

"No. I don't trust anybody who says that there's only one way."

"What were you raised to believe?" Tangerine asked.

Luke sighed. "My mom taught me that believing in yourself is more important than anything. My dad was a recovering alcoholic and tried to believe in a Higher Power for many years. But after she was killed—well, in a way he died with her. No more God, no more Frank. He used it as an excuse to start drinking again. Anyway, his drinking really sucked." Luke rubbed his wrist for a moment. *Suck* didn't even begin to scratch the surface.

Tangerine looked thoughtful. "I can't say that I know exactly what that's like, but I'm so sorry all the same." She paused. "Do you believe in God?"

"I believe in myself," Luke said firmly.

Tangerine lay back. "I believe in love."

Luke felt his heart skip a beat, and they held the silence with their breath.

"So why Utah? Surely you have family, friends in New York . . ."

"Well, Frank and Georgia were both New Yorkers, but they met here." Luke paused. "Here, in fact, on this famous bike trail. They both really loved this part of the world, and we would come some summers and camp. And I guess I feel at home here. These rocks get my head straight better than people."

"And your dad?"

"He's lost. I can't save him. It's strange. I feel sadder about him than I do about my mom. My mom is out there, in here, everywhere. My dad is just . . . well, gone."

eight

"Gin." Ava laid down three kings and the 2, 3, 4, and 5 of spades on the hospital bedside table. Frank nodded and folded. This was their second round. She had bought a pack of cards at the hospital gift shop while Frank was being settled into a room. The ER had been a madhouse, and she had sat with him for two hours in the waiting room, hoping that Charlie would show up. Ava had been amazed when they didn't stop her from going to Frank's room. She didn't even know him! But she'd gone anyway, doing the next right thing. She had even held his hand when they stuck a needle in him for the IV.

Ava looked at the clock on the wall. It was midnight, and she had been AWOL from work for hours. It was closing time, and Sammy probably thought she was on a bender. She should have called him back.

She shuffled and dealt another round. Frank was having a hard time holding his cards and keeping his eyes open.

"Are you sure you want to keep playing?" she asked.

"I need the distraction. My mind is fuzzy and numb. I'm just closing my eyes."

"So did they tell you what kinds of tests they're going to do?"

"Well, I know that I need a biopsy to see the extent of the damage to my liver."

"What about the whole insurance issue?" Ava asked.

Frank had been confused at first about whether he still had insurance. He discarded, and then closed his eyes. "I don't have it. I lost my benefits when I didn't return to work after my bereavement leave. I'm an English teacher. Excuse me, I *was* an English teacher. Not that I cared, then. No wonder Luke left. I can't believe he stuck around for as long as he did."

Ava studied her cards. "Where is Luke now?" Silence. She looked up. Frank was finally asleep. She'd been here before with Nana. Or rather, she hadn't, it was too hard: the treatments, the hand-holding, the worrying.

The cards were splayed across Frank's chest. Ava stood up and leaned over the bed rail to remove them. They were terrible. Was this the hand he was given to play with? Did they both have lousy cards? Was that why they were fucked up? Parentless, childless—it was the same thing. All alone in the world.

Ava sat back down. Now that Frank was asleep, she could really look at him. He didn't look like someone's father. She squinted her eyes and tried to imagine that the figure in the bed was Jim, but she could only see Nana at the end.

She had run away from Nana's suffering and then from Clare's grief, Jim's pain.

· · ·

Ava had gone home to Ohio for Labor Day weekend, after her orientation week but before her freshman year started in earnest. She had had a wild, crazy summer with her job at the Living Room Lounge and her boss supporting her drinking. But that weekend she needed to see if the good girl in her still existed.

Clare met her at the airport alone and blindsided her in the parking lot. They sat in the car without moving.

"Honey, isn't it exciting?" *Exciting* wasn't the word. Ava was shocked.

"What the hell, Clare—this is awful!"

"I didn't expect you to react like this."

"What did you expect?"

"Well, you're so independent. I certainly didn't think that you'd be angry and dramatic."

"What does independence have to do with anything? And how can you say that quitting your job to run a youth hostel in the boonies isn't dramatic?"

"Okay, you're right. It's very dramatic. A huge change."

"So I go off to college and you forget about me? Aren't I a member of this family? Don't I have some say?"

"Listen, honey. You're starting your own life. I have the rest of mine to figure out too. I'm only thirty-five! You and Jim are all I have in the world. I want— I need a fresh start too. Your dad and I haven't had a chance to figure ourselves out, and now we finally have the opportunity."

"You were waiting for Nana and me to get out of the way?"

"Ava. It's not all about you! I've been working nonstop for all of my adult life. I'm burnt out. This is my chance to get out of nursing for a while, work on my poetry. And Jim has been miserable working for someone else. He needs to have his own thing. He'll run the hostel."

"But you're selling the house? Nana just died! This is my home, your home too. How can you sell it?"

"Ava, we need the money to buy the Moonflower."

"But the market sucks right now. You won't get what it's worth." Ava paused. "Can't you change your mind?"

Clare bit her lip.

"Oh, you've already bought this hostel, haven't you? And that's why Jim's not here, right? He's in fucking Moab. I can't believe this."

Clare looked as if she was going to cry, and then she pulled herself together. "I don't know what to tell you, Ava. How to help you. Can we try to have fun this weekend while we pack up the house? Let's just have a good time." Ava wanted to stop her, shake her.

Ava was barely home that weekend. If Clare could do what she wanted, then so could she, and that was partying with a newfound vengeance. And what an excuse! Saying goodbye forever to Ohio, to her old life. Now she was free to permanently alter her reality.

And that was the last time she had seen Clare, almost a year ago. She hadn't seen Jim since they left her in New York.

· · ·

"Luke!" Frank was sitting up in bed, eyes wide in terror, sweat dripping down his cheeks. Before Ava had time to react, a nurse rushed in and pushed him back down, then adjusted his IV drip. Her name tag read "Carmen"—she had taken care of him when they first came in. She was big and soft, twice Frank's size.

"What was that?" Ava asked.

"Night terrors, honey. The worst you can imagine. He your daddy?" Ava shook her head. "Well, it's good you brought him in. I hope he makes it."

"You hope he makes it?" Ava repeated.

"Uh-huh. He's in very bad shape. And we'll have to see the extent of the damage he's done to his liver. He's already got jaundice. See his yellowish tinge?"

Was Frank just going to be written off because he was an alcoholic?

Carmen sighed.

"There's not going to be much we can do for him if he can't stop drinking. Most can't once they've gotten this far. You related?"

Ava shook her head.

"Well, sure is nice of you to sit with him."

"He's not drunk, you know. He's been clean for four days."

"Good for him. But he's still very sick. And it's still nice of you to be here. Sit tight." Carmen patted her on the shoulder as she left.

What were Frank's nightmares about? Ava looked over at him again and fumbled around in her purse. She pulled out her pocket-size version of the Big Book and thumbed through the pages.

There was an inordinate number of mentions of God in the twelve steps of AA, but she was still working on the first step. *We admitted that we were powerless over alcohol and that our lives had become unmanageable.* This idea of powerlessness was beyond her, but she could definitely admit that her life had become unmanageable. She shuddered, remembering.

Here I go again. It's like I keep banging my head against a wall and I wonder why I have a headache. This is so boring. My life is so fucking boring! Why did I let this guy come over? Oh, Jesus, get him off me. How did this happen? This isn't happening to me. Why does this keep happening to me? His tongue is like sandpaper. What happened to my clothes? I hope he likes me! Maybe we'll get married.

It wasn't like that in the beginning. The habitual humiliating, victimizing herself.

She was partying like everyone else in high school. It was a blast. A hangover was a badge of honor. Drinking helped her to not take everything so seriously. All of a sudden one, two, three drinks later she would be popular, the life of the party, beautiful and sexy. *Loved.* Nana was dying, so what? We all gotta go sometime ... And she was naturally tightly wound, so reserved, so shy. Intense. Losing the inhibitions had been like a dream come true, until she didn't know who she was anymore.

Until college, when she couldn't predict what would happen when she drank, what emotions would come up or what crazy things she would do.

"Luke!"

Ava jumped up.

Frank opened his eyes. "Bear."

What? Bare naked? Bear Mountain? Brown bear? *Okay, Charlie. Where the fuck are you? This is getting too weird.*

"Luke?"

"No, Frank, it's Ava. You're in the hospital, Frank."

"I want to be in Moab. Luke is in Moab."

"What?"

Frank's eyes were closed again.

Did he say Moab?

sunday

nine

Luke woke up early, having slept like a rock the night before. He showered and went to the hostel lobby. Nobody was up yet, so he started the coffee and sat down at the desk, looking over yesterday's receipts. He couldn't stop himself from smiling. He and Tangerine had had fun last night. She liked him, he knew it. Brigitte was covering for him, so they were going out on the river today with Cin and Magda. The door banged open, and Hal stumbled in. He looked terrible. His hair was a mess, and his knees were all bloody. Luke checked his eyes to see if there was anything feral about them, but Hal's blue gazed calmly into his brown.

"What happened to you?"

"Coffee first."

"Or how about cleaning yourself up? Are you okay?"

"I just need coffee."

"It's already brewing, man. Now what's up?"

"I got a little freaked out last night, carried away. I'm fine now. Hearing about that girl missing triggered me. I was running away myself, from the Zettians. I ran up the cable by Moonflower Canyon and was running, running. I don't know what happened." Hal poured a cup of coffee. "You ready for some?" Luke nodded, and Hal handed him the cup, pouring himself another one. Luke got milk from the fridge. "Whoa, man. You weren't paying attention this morning. This is strong like Superman," Hal said.

"Superman coffee it is, my friend. You were saying?"

"Yeah, right. Where was I? I fell, and then I was dancing with a bear."

Luke felt a shudder pass through him.

"I must have been dreaming, because I know for a fact that bears don't exist in the canyonlands. The closest they've been seen is the La Sals—but even though it's close, it's a different climate there. Anyway, the miracle is that the bear told me not to worry about the Zettians anymore, not to worry about Bigfoot, and for some reason, I trust her."

Luke didn't answer. *Her?*

"Unbelievable, huh?"

Jesus H. Luke was saved by a few people starting to come downstairs to drink coffee and make plans for the day.

"Wow, Hal" was all he was able to say. *Unbelievable* was right. Luke didn't want to have anything "unbelievable" in common with Hal. He and Hal had both "seen" something bearish. On different nights. Maybe he really was losing his grip.

Luke sipped his coffee, focusing on his senses. Taste: yum. Sound: voices, peals of laughter. Tangerine was coming downstairs with Brigitte and a guest. Sight: two red braids, laughing green eyes, and a smile on her face. The phone rang as Tangerine came up behind him, giving him a quick hug.

"Moonflower Motel," he answered, and turned away, hiding his blush. She kissed him on the ear, and her breath on his skin was too much. He reached out an arm to steady himself on the desk. "I'm sorry, we're booked," Luke managed to stammer, and hung up. He couldn't wait to be on the river with Tangerine.

• • •

Cin showed them how she prepped for a trip: how to pack up a Jeep to bring themselves, the boat, and their supplies to the Fisher Towers turnout; how to load equipment into the boat. Since it was just the four of them for a short trip, they took an inflatable kayak to do the four hours from Fisher Towers to Ida Gulch, where Cin had prearranged their pickup. She showed them the other boats: the J-rig for the biggest rapids, the five-passenger "self-bailing" rowboat, and the paddleboat. She explained safety guidelines and gave them a lesson in wilderness ethics.

It was a lot of information. "I'll probably forget most of it!" Tangerine worried. "But I'm up to it. I learn by repetition."

"I can't believe I haven't done this yet!" Luke said when they were floating in the canyons.

"I can die happy now," Magda said. "I've never white-water rafted before."

"Lady M," Cin said, "I hate to break it to you, but this ain't no white water—this here is the tamest part of the river."

"Oh." Magda looked disappointed.

"It's a great start, Lady M! We can get wilder another time."

Magda looked adorable in her huge sunglasses, floppy hat, and several layers of sunscreen. Even Cin, with her tough bronze skin, had on a couple of layers.

"Oh dear. Well, that just means I'll have to come back! I appreciate this special trip today. I'm due at Mesa Verde in Colorado tomorrow."

Cin laughed. "You can never be too sure! We're pretty good at getting people to change their plans, right, guys?"

"Yes!" Tangerine said. "I'm the perfect example. I could seriously get used to this. What does it take to become a guide?"

"Well, you need training, but anybody can get that. There's a weeklong course up in Jensen that I did. You also need to have a first aid card or be a licensed emergency medical technician. You need to know how to read a map and a compass. But most important, and this is the part that many are lacking, you need to know both how to be a leader and how to be part of a team."

"Are those ants around your ankle your symbols for team-work?" Magda asked.

Cin looked impressed. Luke looked closer. He had never noticed the ants before.

"My mum always called us a team instead of a family!" Tangerine said.

"You have to be yourself first, don't you, before you can be part of a team," Magda mused.

"Amen!" Cin said loudly.

They got down to the business of rafting, quietly enjoying the water, the light undulation of the waves, and the breathtaking scenery. The Colorado River in a raft was definitely the coolest place to be in the summer in Utah. They could put various body parts in the river to cool off, or even jump in, which is what Luke did.

"Aaaahhh!" Splash. He got back into the boat and welcomed the warm air. The canyon walls rose above them as the boat swayed in the water, following the serpentine path of the river. They were sailing by majestic cliff after majestic cliff.

"This is like being in a Salvador Dalí painting," Magda said. She looked like she was half asleep. Luke loved that image. There was definitely something dreamlike about drifting on the water. Why hadn't he made that connection? Dalí was one of his favorite artists. He and Georgia used to go to the Museum of Modern Art regularly just to analyze *The Persistence of Memory*: he closed his eyes and saw the melting clocks, the ants, the cliffs in the background. And *surreal* was an adjective he often heard people use in conjunction with Moab too.

"I met him once, in Paris," Magda continued. "I was very young, and he was as wild and eccentric as his reputation." Wow. Georgia would have loved Magda.

"Well, if you braved Dalí, then we'll have to take you through Cataract Canyon too, Magda," Cin said. "Now those are some white-water rapids. These eddy turns and ferries are nothin'."

"How long would it take?" Magda asked.

"We could do it in a day," Cin said.

Luke raised his eyebrows. "Really? Isn't Cataract Canyon a hundred miles long?"

"I've been offering a day trip," Cin said. "I use a jet boat. It's an extreme experience that not every guide offers, and it's not for the faint of heart. Of course, Luke is right. Most outfitters promote a multi-day trip, including camping and cookouts."

"Is that a dare?" Magda asked, laughing.

"You're ready for it. I know you are."

"Next time," Magda said. "For sure."

Cin took off her float vest and tank top, leaving just her bathing suit on, and jumped into the river. When she climbed back into the boat, Luke saw the tattoos on her lower back: the horse, the tiger, the coyote. On her upper back were the elephant, the blackbird, and there was a new one—a bear.

"You told me all of these animals help you to dream?" Luke's voice was barely a whisper.

"They're all a part of me. You know that I meditate, right?"

"Right."

"Well, that's another form of dreaming for me. I embody their spirits in my meditations."

"That's amazing!" Tangerine traced the bear with her fingers.

"It's my reality."

Luke didn't know what to think. It sounded so out there, so . . . almost Hal. But Hal did drugs. And had a diagnosed mental illness. Luke knew for a fact that Cin never did drugs and was one of the sanest people he had ever met.

"Some of them help me to dream, like the lizard, the blackbird, and now the bear. When I was a kid, I used to have nightmares, *live* a nightmare. I promised myself that when I grew up I would live my dreams. All of these animals protect me—and the people I love too."

Were they having the same dream?

Was Hal?

"Are your tattoos some kind of Native American tribute?" Magda asked.

"Nah. It's completely organic to me. My own cosmology, I guess. Elephants and tigers aren't indigenous to the Americas. But they were in my circus!"

"What made you start collecting tattoos?" Magda asked.

"Well, Solene was a tattoo artist who traveled with the circus when I did, and she got me hooked. Only she wouldn't work on me until I had a sense of purpose. I was running away from myself as well as everybody else, but I had always clicked with animals. I started out as a horse groomer and then was able to convince the owners to let me do stunts on a horse. My horse was named Epona, after the Celtic horse goddess. So this tattoo"—Cin pulled the strap of her swimsuit over her left shoulder—"is of Epona. Solene made me wait six months before she would do it. She wanted me to be totally sure . . . Each of my animals has given me what I needed. At sixteen I needed to feel like I was in charge of my own life, I needed to feel my own authority, and that's what she gave me through Epona."

"Do you want to see my tattoo?" Tangerine asked shyly. *Her too?*

"You've been holding out on me, huh?" Cin said. "C'mon, bare it." Tangerine turned around, pulled up her shirt, and tugged at her bikini.

"I got it while I was in Bali, along with the piercings. I'm a little embarrassed after hearing all of the meaning behind yours. I guess I was just being trendy. I don't even really know what it means."

It was on the small of her back, a Hindu goddess with multiple arms waving.

"Kali." It was a statement, not a question, from Cin. "The creator, and the destroyer. Lead me from the unreal to the real: Kali, the destroyer of unreality. Why, Clem, you're starting your own cosmology."

Luke watched Tangerine readjust herself, beaming at Cin. Lead me from the unreal to the real ... *Why am I seeing bears?*

• • •

Red Rock Rafting Tours's parking lot was empty when they pulled up. Tangerine and Magda went inside while Luke helped Cin unload the van.

"Hey," he said as they backed out the boat. "Your talk about dreaming—I think I was dreaming with you," he tried to joke.

"Oh?"

"Well, I had this weird hallucination up at Angel Rock the other night." They put the boat upright in the supply shed, and Cin gestured for them to sit in a couple of folding chairs toward the back. Luke took this as a sign that he should keep talking. "I had smoked pot with Bruno and Hal earlier." He paused. "It's funny, I saw your new tattoo ... I don't know. It reminded me ... Well, I had an unusual experience with something bearlike."

"You know that I get tattoos of animals after I've experienced them," Cin said quietly. "I've been working with a bear. Or rather, a bear has been working with me."

Luke shrugged. "Well, yeah, I was stoned."

"Well, the question is, what do you want to believe? Do you want to live in a world where things are possible, or in one where they aren't?"

Luke dragged his sandal through the dirt. Could he choose his reality? "I'm a pretty rational guy."

"Okay, so you could rationalize it and blame it on the dope, or you could be open to the mystery, and the possibility that you don't have all of the answers." A car pulled into the parking lot, and Cin stood up. "I'm honored that you shared this with me. I've got a tour to do. Let's keep this conversation open, though, okay?" He stood up too, and she gave him a quick, strong hug. "I love you, you know," she said.

Luke followed Cin inside to say goodbye to Tangerine and take Magda back to the hostel with him.

"Is it time for my siesta?" she asked.

"Absolutely!" he said, trying not to look at Tangerine, who was changing her shirt.

Tangerine finished and turned around. "I'll pick you up at six, and let's go see the sunset!"

ten

The phone was ringing. Ava, in a fog, head pounding, picked it up and slammed it back down. *I'm so hungover.* Had she been drinking?

The phone rang again. "Hello?" she answered this time, eyes blinking rapidly. Wake *up*.

"You really jumped into the next right thing, didn't you?" Charlie. She couldn't find her voice; it was all coming back to her. A drunk dream. The hospital. Moab, Moab, Moab. She had stared at Frank for another half hour last night, willing him to wake up, counting the reasons not to drink. Then she'd headed home and watched TV until her mind was mush and she could sleep. The phone felt alien against her cheek.

"Hello? Are you there?"

"Um, yeah. What time is it?"

"Now? About noon. Ava, my cell phone was turned off! Alec and I went to a movie last night and I forgot to turn it back on. I'm so sorry. I rushed over as soon as I got your message, and I've been with Frank since seven. Can you meet me at Starbucks on 114th in an hour?"

"Yeah, I'll meet you. Sure." Ava hung up the phone and focused her eyes on the dust traveling on a beam of sunlight. What day was it? She looked at the calendar. August eleventh, but it was yesterday's date that was marked in her brain. August tenth. Clare's thirty-sixth birthday. *And I haven't called her in over two months.*

. . .

Charlie had a latte waiting for her. He was wearing a pink button-down oxford-cloth shirt with green shorts and loafers. He always managed to appear so crisp and clean, much younger than he probably was.

"How old are you anyway?" she asked as she sat down.

Charlie pushed the coffee toward her. "I put a Splenda in there," he said. "Thirty-nine."

"I've dated men your age."

"That makes two of us." Charlie winked conspiratorially.

Ava sipped her coffee. "Um, Charlie?"

"Yes?"

"Frank's son, Luke, is in Moab."

Charlie looked surprised. "Yes. Why?"

"My parents are in Moab . . ."

"I didn't know that. Are they on vacation?"

"No, they run a youth hostel."

Charlie stared at her a moment. "Not the Moonflower?"

"Yes, the Moonflower." Ava took another sip of coffee and felt her skin prickle.

"Luke has been living and working there since the end of last year." He held up his cell phone. "The number is right in here. Your dad has probably answered the phone when I called." He laughed. "And it only took us a month to get to this minor detail!"

"This is too freaking weird."

"No, this is why you got sober, making connections like this."

"So?" Ava felt like her head was going to explode.

"So let's go see Frank! Haven't you ever heard of serendipity?"

"Yeah, but . . ."

"Yeah, but now we're caught up in something bigger than we are." Charlie jumped up and held out his hand.

Ava took it and stood. *Something bigger.*

• • •

"Luke!" Frank was writhing in the hospital bed. "Luke! Ursula!" Ava stood in the doorway while Charlie rushed over to Frank and shook him awake. Thank God Charlie was here. The Charlie show. She could just watch. Frank's eyes opened.

"Charlie. The nightmares are terrible—even worse than when I was drunk. Ava . . ." Ava brought two chairs over to Frank's bed and plopped down in one of them. "My angel of mercy." *Yeah, whatever.*

"Do you remember what they're about?" Charlie asked.

"A feral, rabid, huge animal . . . chasing me? Chasing Luke? Luke running from me? Oh, God, I'm toxic."

"You're okay, Frank," Charlie said.

"No. I'm. Not."

No, he's not, Ava thought. "Who is Ursula?"

Frank looked blank. "Ursula? I have no idea. Oh. Luke had a stuffed animal named Ursula." Frank sat up. "What time is it? How long have I been asleep?"

"It's almost two p.m."

"I've got to get out of here. Any chance you brought me clean clothes?"

"Slow down! You're not going anywhere! You haven't even had the liver biopsy yet."

"But the results will take days to get, and I don't need them anyway. I already know that my liver is shot." Frank swung his legs over the side of the bed. "I don't have insurance; it's crazy to be here."

"Yeah, but how shot is the question. And don't worry about the money. C'mon, lie down. You need to rest. Doctor's orders."

"Charlie. You aren't listening. I *know* I need a new liver. And I have to have been sober for six months to even be put on a waiting list."

"The doctor wants you to stay here for a few more days."

"I don't think I've got that kind of time. I just know that I've messed up and now the only thing I have going for me is hope. I've gotta find Luke."

Charlie looked at Ava. "Well, have we got a story for you!"

Ava watched Frank's face light up as Charlie told him.

"Serendipity. I *have* to go now," Frank said. "To Moab."

"Five days sober? Sick from liver damage? Easy does it, first things first," Charlie countered.

"What, are you going to keep me here with AA platitudes?"

"Lie down. Let's just think everything through," Charlie said.

Ava needed a break; she could let them duke it out. "I'm going outside," she said. "Need anything?"

"How about some treats from the Hungarian?" Charlie reached into his pocket and pulled out twenty dollars.

"Coffee too?"

"Definitely."

She walked down the hallway to the elevators. Frank believed that he was going to die, and he didn't want to do so without apologizing to Luke. *Making reparations* . . . repairing a broken relationship. *How do you do that?* What if some things were just too shattered to be fixed?

Why was she so mad at Jim? She brushed that thought aside as the elevator doors opened and she went in. She hadn't seen him since she moved to New York. And that was *his* fault. Her parents called her cell phone, but Jim never said anything of substance, and they never came to New York to *see* how she was doing.

And before she knew it, for the first time that day, she thought about a drink. For a moment, she considered staying in the elevator and going back up. But she could do this. She could walk the three blocks to the Hungarian Pastry Shop without having a drink. She could even go three blocks farther to the Living Room Lounge and officially quit. *Without drinking.*

As soon as she got outside, her feet started walking. Her feet would do the next right thing. Her feet were her Higher Power. She walked toward her former job. When she arrived, she waved at Sammy, hoping that he would come outside. Sure enough.

"What happened to you? I was so worried." All concern. What was she going to say? *C'mon, feet, you brought me here, speak for me.*

"I am so sorry, Sam, that I didn't come back last night. I had to take a friend to the hospital." He looked at her incredulously. He didn't believe her, but he must have known that she was going to quit. She was speaking through her feet. "I'm sorry that I was irresponsible. I should not be working here right now anyway. Goodbye, Sam." Her feet turned and started walking away.

"Ava, wait. It's okay . . . Hey, don't forget to pick up your paycheck next week. And come see me when you feel better." That was easy. *Thank you, feet.*

Cannoli and coffee from the Hungarian. Her feet took her back across the street to St. Luke's. *How funny, feet. Frank's son is Luke, and he's in St. Luke's . . .*

"Cannoli and café au lait to the rescue," Ava said as she walked into the room. Frank was sleeping again, and Charlie was reading a newspaper. "Who won?" Ava passed the brown paper bag to Charlie and dug out the change from her pocket.

"Thanks, sweets. We haven't left yet, as you can see."

"Hey, I stopped by to see Sammy and quit my job."

"Wow. That was a leap of faith, wasn't it?"

"I guess." Ava shrugged. "Now I don't know what I'm going to do."

"Well, I'm proud of you." Charlie opened the paper bag and pulled out a cannoli. "Mmmm . . . sinful. Keep an out-of-work actor company?"

Ava sat back down again. Charlie offered her a cannoli, and she accepted, taking a bite and feeling a rush of sugar so intense that she closed her eyes.

"So what do you think?" Charlie asked.

"It's the best thing ever."

"No, I mean about Moab."

"What about Moab?"

"Going there."

"You mean Frank?"

"I mean you. I mean all of us."

"You are out of your mind."

Charlie smiled.

Ava's heart started beating faster. She couldn't find any more words. Why had her feet led her to this? *Feet, feet, feet, damn my feet!*

"Frank made a convincing argument. He can't go alone, and you—why, the connection is too obvious, the serendipity, the opportunity, your Higher Power . . ."

"My Higher Power? You're supposed to be my sponsor. And this is impulsive. It's, it's . . . it's unsober! It's off the hook. You don't even know what my parents are like—they could be monsters!" She stood up, she had to get away. She felt angry again. It was true, it was true, it was true. She couldn't *not* go. She sat down. But she was not about to get swept up in something beyond her control. She wasn't ready. "I can't do it yet. No." She stood up again. "And how could you take Frank to see Luke? What if it damages both of them even more? I have to get out of here."

"Ava, honey, it's okay. You don't have to do anything that you're not comfortable with. I told Luke when he left that if Frank wanted to get sober, we would go out there looking for him. I never should have let him go. He should have lived with me and finished high school. But I didn't know what the right thing to do was. Thank God Luke landed on his feet."

Ava startled when Frank spoke. "Leave it to Charlie to take on my guilt for abandoning my son."

"You were too sick," Charlie told him.

"That's no excuse, and you know it. You're too soft on me."

"Yeah, I would do just about anything for you."

"I know. I never should have been your sponsor. But I love you anyway." Frank struggled for words. "You both did the right thing. Luke had to leave, and you had to let him go."

"So you're really going?" Ava asked. "When?"

"As soon as we can," Charlie said.

"Damn" was all Ava could say. Her head was reeling.

"Are you okay?" Charlie asked.

"Home. I have to go home. Take a nap."

"'To die, to sleep; to sleep: perchance to dream,'" Charlie said.

"No, I'm okay. Yeah, I need to sleep. I'm confused."

"I was quoting from *Hamlet*. It's normal to be confused, but just keep taking actions and put one foot in front of the other. And remember that you're not alone. Remember who you are."

Who am I? That was a good question. *Hamlet* again? To be, or not to be . . . *And where is home, anyway?*

• • •

Home. Ava was tossing and turning in bed.

Home is where you feel you belong. Do I belong here? In this tiny sublet? Home is where my stuff is . . . Home is Nana's house, where I grew up, so it will always be Ohio . . . Home is where family is . . . But they're in Moab . . . And I've never even been there! And I haven't been feeling very . . . familial. Dreaming, dreaming . . . *Mom!*

Ava bolted upright in bed. *Mom. I want my mommy.* She had been dreaming that she was grocery shopping and that all the food was rotten, that there were no choices, and she was so hungry, and she had called Clare, saying that she was going to slit her wrists if she didn't get something to eat, and Clare had said to her simply, *Why don't you go to another store?*

Her dreams were pulling her back, and she curled onto her right side. *Another store . . . I have to change everything, I have to let go, I can't do this by myself . . .* Ava found herself on a cliff, bright red rocks, purple sun, the abyss below. She screamed at its barrenness. Nowhere to run, nowhere to be. Nowhere, no one, alone. Void. Devoid of humanity. Broken. Unfixable. Jump, jump! Eyes squeezed. I don't want to die and I don't want to live. Not. Like. This. Ssshhhh.

Jump.
Jump into my arms.
I am here.
You are not alone.

What? What? She was enveloped by warm fur, a murmuring voice. Mommy, Mommy, Mom. She was being cradled like a baby. She was a baby.

You are whole and perfect.
You are not a fragment, you matter.
Sleep . . .

eleven

It was almost 6:00 p.m. Luke had been able to get a few hours of work in after the boat trip and was sitting at the front desk, waiting for Clare to take over. He was glad that he had had a chance to talk to Cin. Even though he still didn't know what to believe, it wasn't bothering him as much. And he had a date with Tangerine. He was drumming his fingers against the calendar when the phone rang.

"Moonflower Motel, may I help you?"

"I need to speak to Clare!" came a high-pitched voice. "Is she there? Can you get her for me?"

"Hold on, who is this?"

"It's Jen, I need her, I need her, it's Jen." She went on, her words slurring out fast and sharp, like gibberish.

"Hang on, Jen, it's Luke. I'll go get her." He knocked on the door leading to Clare and Jim's part of the house, but there was no answer. He turned around, and Tangerine was there, smile on her face. "Hey!" Luke said. "Could you do me a favor and find Clare? She must be outside, and Jen's on the phone." Tangerine ran out the door, and Luke picked up the phone again. "Jen?" But the line was dead. Clare came rushing in, Tangerine behind her. "She hung up. I'm sorry."

"What did she say?" Clare asked.

"Well, she sounded high, and she talked a lot, but it was so fast I couldn't catch it."

Clare sighed. "At least she reached out. I haven't heard anything about her since last night, but I might as well call Oswald." She came behind the desk and nudged Luke out of the way. "You two go on. I'm here now, and you might as well go get a bite to eat or something before your hike."

"What do you want to do?" Luke asked as they walked to Jim's Bronco. He tried to shake off a bad feeling. He needed to focus on being with Tangerine. Food. "Want to eat? We have time."

"That yummy ribs place or the diner?"

"Diner," Luke answered. "I've had my fill of ribs for the month. I want pancakes and bacon, with lots of syrup."

They sat in a corner booth at one of the few non-chain eateries in Moab and had breakfast for dinner as Tangerine told Luke about the rest of her day.

"Where do you want to hike?" Luke asked after they had paid the check and were on their way out of the diner.

"Oh, let's get crazy and go up the rim via Cable Arch Trail. By Moonflower Canyon," Tangerine said, grabbing his arm. "That's my favorite spot for the sunset."

Luke's stomach flipped. Her skin, her closeness—and then Hal, Moonflower Canyon, bears, vortexes.

"Crazy it is." Luke steadied himself by looking into Tangerine's smiling eyes. "But we'd better take a flashlight. Jim keeps one in the truck." Luke remembered his initiation up this part of the rim: it was a moonless night, pitch-black. Cin had taken him up there during his first week at the Moonflower. It had been daunting. The last part of the climb was so steep that a rope of cable was attached to the rock. The darkness was immense, and even with a flashlight, it had been difficult to judge distances, drops, how long the cable was . . .

But that January night, looking off the edge into the canyon, Luke felt as if he was staring death in the face. And doing that, for some reason, made him feel more alive.

They got back in the truck and headed toward Kane Creek Road.

Luke let Tangerine climb up the cable first. He was panting by the time he got to the top. The sun's angle on the earth had deepened the color of the rocks to a dark watermelon. The drop into the canyons was spellbinding. The world was vast, unknowable.

He and Tangerine walked across the mesa and silently stopped. They sat down. She leaned against him, so he guessed it would be okay to sneak his arm around her. He couldn't resist smelling her hair. They sat like that for a long time, watching the rest of the sunset. Tangerine wasn't usually this quiet. Luke didn't mind—in a way it made him feel closer to her.

And then Tangerine was kissing him, her lips moist on his, hearts beating fast. And they were holding each other, his face buried in her neck, and there was no time anymore.

She watched them, and waited.
She wanted to tell them about
the girl at the bottom,
but she didn't know how.
A low growl
emerged from her throat.

Luke's eyes fluttered open, and he sat up abruptly. His heart was pounding, but he was feeling a different kind of tension from the one he felt kissing Tangerine. He shook his head.

"Luke, what's wrong?" He didn't want to ruin the mood, but his hallucination had already done that. "Luke, you're flipping me out, what's going on?"

His eyes were shut, fingers rubbing his temples, seeing blood, pain. The nightmare of Georgia's violent death, the image paused in his brain. But it wasn't Georgia slumped over the back of a taxi seat. It was somebody else, at the bottom of the cliff. Jen? He managed to open his eyes and look at Tangerine, reaching out for her hand. He had to speak very slowly, and consider what he said. What was she going to think?

"I don't know why this happened now, but I just had a flash of Jen lying at the bottom of the ravine." The stars were coming out, and Tangerine had her eyes on them. She thought he was crazy. Hell, *he* thought he was crazy. There couldn't be a more unromantic end to their evening.

She finally looked at him. "Well, let's go check it out, shall we?"

Luke realized that he had been holding his breath and exhaled in relief. He felt a strong urge to go to his left, west, so, holding hands, they walked fifty yards to look over the edge of the rocks.

There was a body at the bottom of a sudden drop. Luke felt his stomach lurch.

"Did you bring Jim's flashlight?" Tangerine whispered.

Luke's nod was automatic as he reached into his backpack and pulled it out. He switched it on, scanning. Long dark hair. It was Jen, it had to be, twenty feet or more below.

"What do you think . . ." Tangerine started to ask.

"We've got to get help," Luke said. Neither of them moved.

"I know we've got to get help, but we've also got to see if she's still alive," Tangerine said. "Can we get down there?" Luke couldn't judge the drop. He just wanted to run, make believe he didn't see anything. *Can someone explain to me how I knew where she was?*

"We have to," Luke said, and, without thinking, he turned himself around to hang on to the cliff with his hands on the edge and let go, jumping to the landing. Adrenaline was rushing through him. Tangerine stayed at the top. The body had fallen over a rock with her neck flung back. It was Jen. He picked up her limp wrist and felt for a pulse. Nothing. Panic rose in his throat, and he had to get out of there, couldn't be with the dead body for one more second. And there was no way that he could pull her out.

And then he found himself back up with Tangerine, looking down at Jen. How did he do that? How much time had passed?

"Dead?" Tangerine asked him, face pale in the moonlight.

"No pulse. Look at her. Neck snapped."

Why had he been led to her? He felt dizzy and forced himself to turn away.

"Let's go," Tangerine whispered. Yes. He had to reorient himself to find the right markers to go back down the rock face, and they scrambled among the stones faster than they thought possible. He looked at the clock on Jim's dashboard. It was around 11:00 p.m. Luke started driving down Kane Creek Road, toward town. He couldn't get the image of Georgia out of his head.

"Did I really say that there was no pulse?" he asked Tangerine. She nodded slowly. "How did I get back up?"

"Um ... you climbed?" They were both quiet for a moment, and then Tangerine said, "I'll pray for her."

"But she's already dead."

"It doesn't matter." Praying. She'd never mentioned that before. "Where should we go?"

Death hovered, she could smell it.
Her paws moved over the girl's torso.
Her head lowered.

She rose up on her haunches.

Her head lowered again.

Luke and Tangerine decided to go straight to the police station and have Oswald, or whoever was on duty, call Jen's parents. They drove past Cin's trailer on Kane Creek Road but didn't stop—Cin didn't have a phone. Luke saw flames out of the corner of his eye, and Tangerine turned around in her seat.

"Did you see Cin?" Tangerine whispered. Luke shook his head. "She was sitting by the fire with her eyes closed and didn't even flinch when we passed."

"Must have been meditating."

Tangerine craned her neck around again. "I guess."

• • •

Luke shivered, sitting in the lobby of the police station. Why did he feel so cold? Tangerine's hand felt warm on his thigh. Wasn't she cold? Oswald finally shuffled over to them. He was talking, but Luke couldn't hear what he was saying, he just saw Oswald's lips moving.

The girl moaned softly
and opened her eyes.
They looked.
Looked. Mouth turning
up. Eyes down.
Life.

The time between giving the report at the station and hovering above the canyons in a helicopter was missing from Luke's memory, but here they all were. Oswald had marshaled people pretty quickly. The police had a protocol for everything, even people falling off cliffs. EMTs, sheriff's deputies with flashlights, and Carson's helicopter. Jen's mother had needed a sedative. Her father had a face as cold as stone, staring straight ahead. Everybody but the sheriff's deputies crammed into the helicopter, its beacon guiding them. Luke and Tangerine at least would have to be driven back by the deputies so that there could be room on the helicopter for Jen's body, carried on a stretcher.

Carson didn't need to ask for directions. It was good that the moon was full. Within minutes they were over the mesa—such surreal, dreamlike beauty—searching for Jen's body. This was right. Luke needed to be there. He needed to see. He scanned the ground below, and within seconds, his eyes landed on her.

• • •

Jen was not in the same position. She had moved.

• • •

This was impossible. Everyone else was ecstatic. Jen was breathing, Jen was alive . . . They were being driven back to the hostel, he could hear the chattering around him. Luke should have been happy, but all he could think was, *Why isn't Georgia alive? Why did Georgia have to die?*

The EMTs had found Jen lying on her side, and she was breathing. There had to be an explanation. Luke had to have made a mistake.

monday

twelve

"Hi, my name is Ava, and I'm an alcoholic."

"Hi, Ava," the room said back to her.

"A lot has happened in the past couple of days. I had a good reason not to be here yesterday. I was sleeping! I can't remember a time when I've slept so well. I feel great." It wasn't her business to talk about Frank, was it? She still needed to make sense out of it. "And I saw my sponsor, quit my job, and slept some more." After her nap yesterday, she had gotten on the Internet, looking up flights to Moab. There was a special: $199 round trip from JFK to Salt Lake City. Then she spent the rest of the evening researching Moab itself. She had had no curiosity about it before. What had compelled her parents to move there? Maybe she *should* go. Maybe there was something to this serendipity. "I think I'm starting to get it," Ava continued. "If I act as if my life doesn't suck, maybe that's the way to get it to stop sucking."

If she left before she changed her mind. If she left with Charlie and Frank. If she left with this strong urge to feel . . . at home. Funny, it was almost as strong as the urge to drink, to fill herself up. Maybe it would be crazy not to go.

After the meeting she went out for coffee with some other AAers and ended up telling them everything.

"Do it," one guy said.

"Don't do it," said another.

"Why?" Ava asked.

"It's too much change. It might trigger you to drink."

"I'm sure there are meetings out there. Besides, my sponsor will be with me. And I'm finally getting a clue about how self-centered I've been."

There. She had made up her mind.

• • •

"Can you bring some liquid cleaner? We've run out here, and this place is a pigsty," Charlie said to Ava when she called, then gave her Frank's address. Frank had managed to get himself discharged the night before.

"I'll be there soon." She walked up to 121st Street, stopping at the drugstore and at an ATM to see how broke she was. She had $483.74 in the account she used to pay her living expenses. She'd better go to Moab sooner rather than later, so she could come back and get another job before school started. She would go for a week; they all would. The question was, How soon? Today? Tomorrow? *Just keep doing the next right thing and more will be revealed.* She'd never been farther west than Ohio. *Am I actually excited?*

She was the one, after all, who had refused to visit Jim and Clare on holidays, who'd insisted that she was "fine," that she had "work" to do, who'd kept her contact with them to a bare minimum. Maybe Jim would offer to pay some of her room and board again. Maybe she wouldn't be so stubborn. She wanted to keep the bounce in her step. She bounced over to Frank's and rang the doorbell, waiting a few seconds before she was buzzed into the building.

"I'm going to Moab with you," she said to Charlie when he opened the door. He was exhausted, but the place looked spotless.

"I knew you'd come around!"

"I even found flights for a hundred and ninety-nine dollars!"

"That's unheard of! Go say hi to Frank. I've put him in Luke's room while I clean his. This place hasn't been cleaned since Luke left."

Ava looked around. "Great job. Will you come and clean my place next?"

"He's in there." Charlie motioned to an open door.

Frank looked worse than yesterday, if that was possible. He really could be dying. Was this a bad idea? Charlie had said on the phone that Frank was discharged against medical advice and that his prognosis was grim. She didn't want to think about that. What had he said? That hope was the only thing he had going for him? She looked around the small room, which had beautiful high ceilings and walls entirely covered with bookshelves and vibrantly colored paintings.

"So, Frank," Ava said, "when do you want to go?"

"As soon as possible," he said.

After Charlie was finished cleaning, he got on Frank's computer.

"I can get us flights to Salt Lake City as soon as tomorrow," Charlie said. "I have my credit card ready. Shall we do it?"

"Yes!" Frank and Ava both called out.

"Hot damn! That part was easy," Charlie said.

"I can't believe we're doing this. What about your work?" Ava went to the living room doorway and looked at Charlie.

"Work shmurk. So I miss an audition or two. My agent will be sending you a gift basket, grateful that I'm not camped out on her doorstep as usual."

"What about Alec?" Ava asked. Was Charlie in love with Frank?

"He has an important project coming up and will be working around the clock anyway. If I'm out of his hair, he won't have to feel guilty for working so much."

"Talk about carpe diem then."

"That's exactly what I'm talking about."

"Hey," Frank croaked. "Don't forget to rent a car."

"I know, I know. I reserved that at the same time as the e-tickets. It's all taken care of. We have a noon flight. Four, no, *five* hours of flying—oh, and it's in the mountain time zone, so it's two hours earlier—then four and a half hours of driving. We should be there by eight p.m." Charlie came over to look at Frank, who was still in bed. "Should we give them a heads-up?"

"What do you mean, call them? I don't know about Ava, but surprise is the only leg I have to stand on with Luke. He may not want to see me, I realize, but I have to try." Frank looked at Ava. "If you tell your parents, keep me a surprise."

"I'm not going to tell them anything."

"Okay. So I'll book the two of us at the Moonflower under an alias," Charlie said, fingers hitting the computer keys. "Ava, you'll stay with your parents, right?"

"That's why I'm going," she said. "Jim and Clare will figure something out, after they get over the shock."

"That's the spirit! Okay, Frank, I know that we should leave you to rest, but I called a few people this morning and asked them over for an impromptu meeting." Charlie looked at his watch. "They're coming in a half hour."

"Who?" Frank asked.

"That remains to be seen . . . Right now I'll do a sandwich run. Any requests?"

• • •

"So, who painted all of these?" Ava asked after Charlie left, gesturing to the art on the walls.

"That's mostly Luke's work."

"Wow. He's amazing. The colors and shapes on those two remind me of Picasso."

"He would love that compliment," Frank said. "The only painting Luke took was the portrait that his mother painted of him when he was a little boy."

Interesting choice, Ava thought. She sat down and studied the paintings so that she wouldn't have to look at Frank.

"Have you started working on the steps yet?" he asked.

"I'm still on the first one. I don't even know why I'm here. I don't know whether I'm coming or going."

"Here literally or here cosmically?"

"Both, I guess." Ava stared at a painting. What was it meant to be? She kept seeing different things in the patterns: a face, an apple, an animal?

"How did you get here? I mean, what made you willing to try AA?" Frank asked.

"Dumb luck?" As Ava spoke she kept her eyes on the painting. "I thought that if I solved my problems with life, I wouldn't need to drink so much, and believe me, I tried everything, even a therapist for a few weeks . . . I stopped seeing her as soon as she mentioned I might be an alcoholic and suggested meetings, but then I would still find myself in stupid situations with the common denominator being alcohol, and I would think about AA . . . Then I thought that once I stopped drinking, my problems would be solved. But now it's like the opening of Pandora's box. I had no idea it would be this hard to stay sober. But something is working . . ."

She finally looked at Frank. He hadn't managed to stay sober.

"It's grace, Ava. It has to be," Frank said.

"Okay, Frank. Here's the thing about all of this Higher Power / God / grace stuff. Do you really have to believe in God to stay sober?"

"How have you stayed sober for fifty some days?"

"Sixty! Meetings, I guess. Charlie." She laughed. "My feet! My feet have known where to go, even when my mind doesn't."

"Okay then. Your feet are your God du jour."

Ava raised her eyebrows. "God du jour?"

"Yeah, it's rare to have a spiritual awakening that's like a lightning bolt. We're both in early sobriety. Most of us don't believe in a power greater than ourselves at this point. How could we? Besides booze or drugs? God du jour is whatever works to keep you sober and on the right path. Ava, trust me. I was successfully sober for eighteen years. The reason I slipped is that I lost my faith."

Frank handed Ava a piece of paper from the table by the bed. "Write down a list of everything God is *not.*" She raised her eyebrows, and Frank looked at her pointedly. "Start with your parents." Ava leaned over the coffee table with the piece of paper. Okay, she could do this. She wrote: *My God is not Jim, Clare, men, sex, drugs, rock 'n' roll—* she smiled—*it is* not *booze, nightclubs, popularity, anger, frustration, a job, school, my weight, the gym.*

"Yeah, that's pretty cool. I think I get it."

"Now that you know what your vision of God isn't, maybe you can be more open to what your vision of God is. For instance, my God of today is you."

"Me?"

"Yes, you. You got me to the hospital; it can't be a coincidence that my son is working for your dad. And your God du jour is your feet, doing the next right thing, taking you where you need to go. You go to meetings, quit your job, listen to Charlie . . . Well, we've both got Charlie on our side . . ." And, as if on cue, Charlie opened the door, with a grocery bag in his hand and two men and one woman right behind him.

"Looks like the meeting has already started!"

Ava rolled her eyes at Charlie's exuberance. Frank looked incredulous. He was bombarded with hugs, kisses, and pats. Ava stood up and walked over to help Charlie with the food.

"Is anybody hungry?" Charlie called out. His friends waved him off. Charlie gave Ava a plate and a turkey sandwich. "This is some of Frank's sober class from nineteen years ago," he explained.

"So this is like a high school reunion?"

Charlie laughed. "You could call it that. Sometimes AA does feel like high school. Not so great having to go through all of that teenage angst again."

• • •

After Frank's friends said their goodbyes, Charlie and Ava left Frank to get some rest and walked into the park on Riverside, strolling down the bike path to the first level, and then under the highway to the river. They were quiet until they got to the promenade and sat on a bench.

"I love summer in New York," Charlie said. "I don't mind the heat at all. The city empties out, and I can feel like it's really my own. Not too shabby for an Oklahoma boy."

"So I'm curious. All of this hoopla for Frank. Were you in love with him?" Ava asked.

Charlie looked surprised. "Is this hoopla? Really? Let me think about your question. Frank was pretty damn cute back in the day, so when I was the one deep in my addictions, it was more like hero worship, and I wanted him to be my daddy. It sure helped get me sober. I wanted him to be impressed with my progress. Seriously. That's not real love, though, is it? And I admired his relationships with his wife and son. I wanted what he had. It broke my heart when Georgia died and he started drowning in his pain. It broke my heart that Luke felt he had no option but to leave. What's your dad like?" Charlie asked gently, abruptly. It was Ava's turn to be startled.

"He's everybody's best friend. And everybody loves him. You'll love him," Ava couldn't help adding sarcastically. She looked across the river to New Jersey.

"Pain is pain, sweetheart. And it's your pain. It doesn't mean that it's any less valid than mine, or Frank's, or anybody else's."

"And the awful thing is that I really want my dad to be proud of me and to like me, but I'm afraid he won't."

They sat in silence for a while, Charlie rubbing her back.

"We drunks seem to have a hard time accepting any love that isn't the perfect fit. I couldn't experience love and friendship until I got sober. I couldn't feel the love from my parents either. It's only now that I know for sure they do love me, in their own way. Which doesn't happen to be my way. And we get to find out what stuff we're made of."

thirteen

Luke woke to a rap on his screen door. He managed to yell out "Just a minute!" and sat up in bed, disoriented. He didn't have time to think. Tangerine opened the door and came in. At least he was wearing underwear.

"I brought you a cup of coffee," she said.

Luke blinked and smiled weakly, reaching for the T-shirt he had worn yesterday.

"Clare made muffins, but she said you have to come get them yourself, and Magda wants to say goodbye to you," Tangerine continued.

On second thought . . . Luke stood up, opened his bureau, and pulled out a green T-shirt. He should have asked her to wait, but he didn't know how. She wasn't looking at him anyway. Well, she was in a sense. She was looking at the painting. He put on his jeans.

"Is that you?" she asked.

He nodded.

"That's a gorgeous painting."

"My mother liked her reds." Here they were, talking like nothing had happened. Tangerine handed him the coffee and stood there, entranced by the painting. She had braided her hair into pigtails again, and the freckles on her nose crinkled as she smiled.

"What time is it?" he asked as he took a sip of the coffee. "What day is it?"

Tangerine had remembered that he liked milk and sugar.

"It's eleven a.m. Monday. Congratulations. You got six hours of sleep."

Luke had slept fitfully but also dreamed deeply. Was he hunting for a bear, or with a bear?

"Let's go outside," he said, setting down his coffee, opening the door, and pulling out two chairs. Tangerine followed. He went back in for his coffee, and when he returned, Tangerine was sitting with her legs stretched out and eyes closed, pretending to be asleep.

"I slept so-so. What about you?" Luke said as he sat down.

Tangerine shook her head. "Like the dead! Uh-oh. Poor choice of words. Even with all that excitement and drama. First, that fantastic kiss . . . then, well, you were there . . ."

There it was on the table. Everything about last night was crazy and needed to be talked about, but all he could think of was touching her, kissing her. He knew that he had to say something; the silence was unbearable. He could feel his palms sweating. What should he say? She was looking at him to gauge his reaction, and he was speechless. So he leaned over and he kissed her. It was awkward; his mouth almost missed hers because she wasn't expecting it. It sent her into peals of laughter. Then she got up and sat in his lap and started kissing him. Again.

Luke still hadn't had time to think about the other events of last night when he and Tangerine finally walked into the hostel and were overwhelmed with questions from Jim, Brigitte, Bruno, and Magda.

"How did you find her?"

"Was she really dead?"

"Were you totally freaked out?"

"Did you touch her?"

"Did she say anything to you?"

"Did she mention a bear?" Luke hadn't even noticed Hal in the room.

"Whoa. Slow down, guys!" Tangerine said. "I can't explain it. We were just hanging out when"—*don't tell them about my weird vision*—"Luke wandered to the edge of the mesa and saw Jen lying at the bottom of the rocks." *Thank you, Tangerine.* Luke remembered seeing the image of his mom again and sucked in his breath.

"How did you get down there and up again? Isn't it a long drop?" Brigitte asked.

"I don't remember."

"Well, it's as if we were meant to find her. Maybe we had help, if you know what I mean." Tangerine looked triumphant. *No, there's got to be a logical explanation for that.* "It's a miracle!"

"Tange, I'm not sure I couldn't get a pulse. Maybe I didn't find the right spot. I must have been wrong. Everything happened so fast."

Tangerine looked shocked by his words. "She was dead. She had no pulse," she insisted.

"That's so cool, man. Death to life. When does that happen?" Bruno said lightly.

Luke shook his head. "It's just not logical, Tange. It's impossible."

"I know what I saw. It's a miracle."

"Okay. Okay. Sorry. You're right." *Your belief is your reality. It's just not mine.* "It's a miracle she survived that drop." The tension was palpable.

"Oh, you two," Magda said. "What an adventure! I wish I had been with you."

"According to Carson, if you guys hadn't found her, she really would be dead," Jim said. "Clare's at the hospital now with Jen's parents, waiting for the full prognosis."

The bear, the hospital, Georgia . . . and now Tangerine was mad at him for being an Unbeliever. *Would somebody please change the subject?* Luke didn't want to talk about it anymore.

"Did we have a lot of people check out this morning?" he asked Jim. He was hoping there wouldn't be too much work to do.

"Yes, actually, quite a few. The only one left is Magda."

"I guess that's my cue," Magda said.

"Oh, we wish you weren't leaving!" Jim said.

"I'll be back someday, I promise! Goodbye, Luke. I enjoyed my time with you so much." Magda's eyes pierced through him, and he almost jumped away when she reached out for a hug.

Luke opened the front door for her after she had refused his help with her bag. Clare was coming toward them.

"You weren't gone long," he said as she walked in.

"Well, Jen was sleeping, and I got all of the information I needed. She'll survive, and although she's in bad shape, she didn't break any bones," Clare said. "They can't understand it. But her bloodstream is full of so much crystal meth. I don't know." She looked at Luke. "Is it possible that she didn't fall?"

"Yes," Luke said at the same time that Tangerine said, "No."

"I saw her body draped over a rock as if she had fallen," Tangerine said. "And Luke said she was dead."

"Her parents were glaring at me," Clare continued. "I feel terrible. She reached out to me, and I failed her."

"Hold up. How's that?" Luke asked.

"She told me about Jaime. If only I had answered the phone when she called . . ."

"Wait a second, Clare." Jim put his arm around his wife. "This isn't your fault. You told Oswald everything you knew—Jaime, the phone call."

"I need to go be alone for a while. Can everybody hold down the fort?" She didn't wait for an answer before heading up the stairs.

Silence. "Okay," Jim finally said. "I'm going to try to turn a piece of wood into a Kokopelli. Or maybe I should change my kachina. Luke, you're on the schedule for the front desk. Are you okay with that?"

"If Tangerine can take over the cleaning, I can watch the desk for a couple of hours until Carlos picks me up to go to Grand Junction," Brigitte said. Luke was relieved. He couldn't deal with the front desk right now.

"No worries. Red Rock is closed today," Tangerine said as she headed upstairs without looking at Luke.

"Great," Jim said. "I'll be in the studio if anyone needs me." And he left.

"Thanks, Brigitte, I owe you one," Luke said. Then he followed Jim to his studio and watched him sit down at his table and pick up a piece of wood. "Jim, can I talk to you for a minute?" he asked.

Jim looked up from the wood. "What is it, son?"

Luke felt blown off course by that last word. He wanted to talk about his mother and the way she had died, her body position, so similar to Jen's, but he felt a huge lump in his throat.

"Luke?"

Okay. What did he *need* to say? As opposed to all of the things he wanted to say. If he didn't speak, his head would explode. "I was wrong. She wasn't really dead—she couldn't have been."

"It's okay, Luke. It's still a miracle that you found her. You still saved her life."

"Tangerine insists that she was dead."

"I believe both of you."

125

"How can you?"

"People can see different things in the same situation, Luke. You know that. We all see the world through our own experience." Okay. He could handle that. "Don't worry, Luke."

Luke realized he had been holding his breath. He felt a sting in his eyes. "Thank you," he mumbled, but he still hovered in the doorway. "Can I borrow the truck?"

"No problem. Where are you going?"

"I don't know yet . . . maybe back up the rim to investigate."

"The light of day can bring clarity. Want some company?"

"No, thanks. I really need to be by myself for a little while. Then I'll be more useful when you need me later."

"And you will be needed." Jim handed him the keys, and Luke went to his trailer to get his backpack. As an afterthought he grabbed the kachina doll from where he had stuffed it.

He drove past the hospital onto Kane Creek Road, past Cin's trailer to the turnout back to Cable Arch Trail and Moonflower Canyon, the sense of urgency growing. He parked haphazardly, abruptly, slamming the door as he got out, running to find the crevice. He was sweating as soon as his arms and legs started working, pulling him up the rocks. It felt good. But how could somebody high on crystal meth climb up here?

He reached the mesa. The landscape itself hadn't changed. Did he think it would? He looked over the edge of the cliff. How had he climbed down and then back up? He sat on the rim and turned around, dropping, hugging the edge with his body and gripping the top with his hands. Subtracting his height, he had about fourteen feet to go. If he landed wrong . . . *Don't think about it.*

He let go and felt all the blood rushing to his head. He yelled in pain as his feet hit the ground. *Damn.* But he was in one piece. He sat for a moment, orienting himself. Jen had been over . . . there.

Okay. I got down. Now if I can just get back. He looked up twenty feet. It *was* steep. But last night, he hadn't thought about it, he'd just done it. And, it didn't look as steep from here as it did from the top. He saw crags where he could put his feet and hands. Not so impossible after all. He fumbled in his backpack for his bottle of water and took a long drink. When he put the bottle back, he noticed the kachina on the ground. It must have fallen out. He would leave it. Maybe it wanted to be here. Or it could become somebody else's talisman. He picked it up and propped it against the cliff wall.

The climb back up was satisfying, and he was able to appreciate the barren beauty of the sandstone as he made his way across the mesa and down to the parking lot. He felt like himself again.

Luke drove past the hospital and saw Cin's old Jeep in front. And there was Clare's Camry too. He parked next to Cin's car. They must be visiting Jen. He'd stop in and say hello.

When he got to Jen's room, Cin and Clare were sitting on the floor outside, deep in conversation.

"Hey, guys."

"Cool Hand Luke!" Cin jumped up, grabbed his hand, and squeezed it. "You're a hero. I was hoping to see you."

"Well, I saw your cars, thought I'd come in. Clare, weren't you just here?"

"Kerri called to apologize for giving me the cold shoulder, so I came back," Clare explained. "Jen's still unconscious. I want to be here when she wakes up."

"Is she really going to make it?" Luke peered inside and saw the bed and Jen—white sheets and chestnut hair. In a chair was her mother, shock still on her face.

"We hope so," Clare said.

"Do they know what happened yet?"

"Jen's the only one who can tell us, unless someone comes forward. It makes me miss Ava even more. I bought myself a ticket to New York for a late birthday present. I'm leaving on Thursday." For some reason that made Luke feel both better and worse.

He hadn't talked to Charlie in a while and wondered how Frank was doing. He felt his chest begin to tighten.

"Luke, are you okay?" Cin asked.

"Uh, yeah." He blinked the tears away.

•   •   •

They were in the common room of the hostel, and it was almost 10:00 p.m. Luke was working on a crossword puzzle and half listening to conversations on either side of him. One of them was Bruno telling a guest of his plans to transfer to the Recreation Resource Management Program at the community college. Tangerine was talking with Brigitte about missing her family. "I have to go home soon. This experience has made me feel more alive, more aware of my responsibilities . . ." She couldn't stop talking about the night before. Her perception wormed its way into every conversation. Responsibilities for what? Would they be able to get past their philosophical differences? Was it really that important when she was just going to leave anyway?

Brigitte yawned. "Oh! I'm sorry . . . I need to get some shut-eye. Good night, guys," she said. Luke studied the crossword more intently. Things needed to get back to some kind of normal.

"Um, Tange?"

"Yeah?"

What was he going to say? He let the words come out of his mouth. "Are you tired?"

"A little bit."

"We have to kick ourselves out of here pretty soon. Do you

want to hang out in my trailer?" He said it and tried not to hold his breath.

"Yes!"

• • •

It was hot inside the trailer.

"Maybe we should sit outside, out of the heat?"

Tangerine shook her head no.

"Are you tired?" Luke said.

"You already asked me that."

"Well, I'm tired," he said.

"You want to lie down?" Tangerine asked.

"You?" She nodded, and they crawled onto the little bed together, lying on their sides, noses almost touching. Her breath on his cheek was tantalizing. They lay there together, not saying anything.

"It's okay, Luke," Tangerine whispered. Was he dreaming that he was kissing her? "Fact is stranger than fiction, and let's just leave it at that."

And his lips found hers, soft and warm.

tuesday

fourteen

"This is amazing!" Ava couldn't believe her eyes. She was on the highway in a rental car with Charlie and Frank, approaching Moab, watching maroon rocks loom in the distance and mountains rise as they got closer and closer.

"You haven't seen anything yet. You want to go the scenic route?" Frank said. "This is the turnoff for Moab, but if we keep going, just ahead there's a little town called Cisco. Turn right off the interstate and we'll follow a road along the Colorado River, then meet up with U.S. 191." Charlie made the turn, and they gasped at the first canyon they entered. Mountains of sandstone overwhelmed them.

"What are all those spires?"

"That's called Fisher Towers," Frank said. "We're lucky to be driving through here so late in the day, with the sun just low enough to cast all those shadows and shapes. Look. These formations were created by erosion—wind and water—millions of years ago. Isn't it the inverse of everything we know in New York? You know what I mean?"

Ava was too stunned to answer.

"Energy is here in spite of the decay," Frank said. "You notice not only how the stones are carved, but how the stones themselves carve the sky."

"It's like Mars or something" was all Ava could say.

• • •

In Moab, Ava stared. This strip mall of a town could be anywhere in America. Charlie kept driving on U.S. 191, and they saw the supermarket, the Ford dealership, and the last gas station before leaving town.

Ava looked at the directions Charlie had printed off the Internet. "After that gas station, take the first left and you'll see a sign reading 'Moonflower Motel.' Oh! I see it! There."

Charlie took the left and parked the car, and Ava got out. She stopped short. What a scene. It was almost dark, but there seemed to be gobs of people. She heard Charlie and Frank walk up behind her.

"What the hell?" She felt Frank turn from her, and she also moved her head toward the voice. Then Frank crumpled to the ground.

• • •

"What the hell?" It couldn't be. This was lunacy. Why now? Luke was just starting to figure things out. Frank was helped back up by this Amazonian blonde—who was she? His arms were stretched out, pathetic—what did he want? Chaos. Chaos inside and outside Luke's head. Clare screaming "Ava!" *What?* Luke stood there, unbelieving. Tangerine put a hand on his elbow. They had been hanging out at the picnic tables.

He squeezed his eyes shut, hoping Frank was an apparition that would disappear. If he didn't believe, then it wouldn't be true. He opened his eyes and saw Charlie behind his father in the shadows. "No." *I can't fucking deal with this. They're here for what? To take me back?* "No."

Charlie came forward. "Luke."

134

That was it. He wrenched his arm away from Tangerine and took one step closer to Frank.

"Is he for real?" Luke focused his attention on Charlie. He couldn't look at Frank. "You bring him here, looking like this, after all he's done?"

Charlie nodded. "I keep my promises."

"Oh, he's sober, is he?" Luke said, his voice dripping sarcasm. "I am so out of here." He turned around and started walking toward his trailer.

"Luke!" Charlie's voice. He kept walking. "Luke, he's sick. He could be dying." Was that supposed to be the drama to pull him back in? Pathetic. *He's already dead to me.* Enough with the resurrections.

· · ·

Ava was hugging Clare. And it was nice to feel like she didn't want to let go. Clare had a ticket to go see Ava. They were connected. Clare was crying, and whispering, "Baby, my baby," over and over again. When did she ever call Ava "baby"? Ava couldn't have imagined a better reception. Poor Frank. Everything had happened so fast. No chance to get their bearings. Frank falling. The second she had lifted him up, she'd heard Clare scream her name and moved into another world. She had known that Luke would flip—anybody would. She wasn't quite ready to face Jim yet, but at least this was all on her own terms. Luke was being blindsided.

She felt a hand rest tentatively on her shoulder. "I'm glad you're here." Was Jim crying? But she wouldn't let go of Clare. That was enough for now.

"Are you okay?" Ava asked, and Clare laughed.

"Aren't I supposed to be asking you that?" Clare pulled back slightly, so that she could touch Ava's face. They both needed a mother.

Luke was finding it difficult to breathe. He ripped open the door to his trailer and stood there blinking the tears away. He grabbed his duffel and stuffed the clothes he had recently unpacked back in. His sleeping bag was all rolled up, so he took that too. He looked up. The painting. He couldn't take it with him. He needed even less stuff this time. It was nice that he had hung on to his five-year-old self for as long as he had. *Goodbye.* He cut through the thicket to avoid the hostel, parking lot, people. He made it up to the highway in the dark, then flipped on his flashlight. He looked right, and then left. Right on the highway was into town. Left on the highway was nothingness for fifty-four miles until Monticello. He chose left.

• • •

"Oh, Ava. I've missed you so much. I can't believe you're here. How?"

"Happy birthday?" Ava said. "Surprise? And the how is over there." Charlie and Frank were sitting at a picnic table. Jim was talking to them, of course. He talked to everybody. "The short answer is that Frank is Luke's father."

"What?"

"It's a long story. I'll introduce you. Frank doesn't look too good." Ava pulled Clare over with her, toward her own father. Did they really live here? With all of these people coming and going? God, she would go insane!

"Do you need a place to stay?" Jim was saying.

"We actually have reservations." Charlie smiled at Ava.

"But I'm not sure we should stay here after Luke's reaction," Frank said.

"Of course you should stay. Luke's had a big shock. In fact, I would have bolted too. But he'll come around. Stay. Please."

How did Jim do that? How did he lighten up serious situations so easily?

"Well, I see you've met Jim. Are you okay, Frank?" she asked.

"I know that I'm doing the right thing, no matter how selfish it seems. I'm not here to make him come back with me. If that's how it appears . . ."

"I don't think he even knows what to make of it," Jim said.

Ava could feel Jim's eyes on her. But was he seeing her?

"How did you all come here together?" Jim asked. Charlie and Frank were both looking at her, waiting for her to answer.

"Well, Jim, Clare," she said, bracing herself. "They've been helping me get sober."

"Sober?"

She looked at Jim sideways to see how it was sinking in.

"Since when do you have an alcohol problem?" The anguish on his face was strangely satisfying.

"For three years. Since Nana got sick."

"You never asked us for help," Clare whispered behind her.

"I didn't know how to. You guys had your own grief to deal with, and I thought alcohol *was* helping me. And then you guys left."

"You were a straight-A student, always so sure of yourself. I can't believe this," Jim said.

"Well, the good news now is that she is letting go of that persona and asking for help," Charlie intervened, with a look that said *I've been here before.*

"I guess we were wrong about that—me being able to take care of myself."

Clare reached for Ava's shoulders and turned her around. "Let me take you upstairs. We have a lot of catching up to do."

"Yes."

Clare steered her toward the door. Jim didn't move.

"Good night, Ava," she heard Charlie say softly. She knew he understood who she was.

• • •

The air felt sharp in Luke's chest. *What am I doing? Where am I going?* Screams stuck in his throat. A boulder loomed large on the side of the road, and he ran, smashing himself into it, the pain finally allowing a wretched sound to erupt from his gut. He felt as if he could cry forever. He had held himself together for so long. Why did he have to deal with this at all? He had moved on. *I'm freaking over it already!* He heard a car coming and instinctively turned away from the road. He heard the wheels slowing to a halt. *Oh shit, don't be them, don't be them.*

"Luke." It was Jim's voice. "Get in." Luke shook his head. "Then I'm coming out."

Luke slid down the rock and sat on the ground. Jim got out of the car, sat next to him, and, pointing at his bags, said, "What's this?" Luke shrugged. "Running, running. You don't have to run anymore, Luke."

"Well, I'm not going with them."

"I don't think they're here to take you anywhere."

"Oh." Luke's mind was splitting apart. "I'm not thinking straight. I just can't deal with this right now."

"He's pretty sick."

"*Dying* is what Charlie said. He probably pickled his stupid liver. That's why I left him! I knew this was going to happen, and I didn't want to watch."

"Okay. I get that."

"It's sadistic."

"I don't know about that, but it's pretty weird, huh? My daughter and your father waltzing in together?"

Luke didn't say anything.

"To top it off, I was told that the three of them met in AA."

Luke could hear disbelief in Jim's voice. "I guess that's pretty strange. She still mad at you?"

"She must be." Jim was silent for a moment. "I was trying so hard not to be like my own dad. Authoritarian, abusive, critical, and yes, a drunk. I was more than grateful to have her grandmother be the parent, so I could be her friend. I didn't want to worry about her. And now that she's here, what do I do?" Jim said, more to himself than to Luke.

"Well, why aren't you back there with her?"

"That's complicated. One, I'm terrified. I want to make it all right with her and I'm afraid of screwing that up too, and scaring her away. Two, I was worried about you. I don't want you to run away again. You're too important to us."

"Yeah." Luke nodded. He could feel the tears coming back. "But I'm making a new life here. If he really loved me, he would leave me alone."

"Maybe he just wants to say that he's sorry."

"I've moved on," Luke said.

"Have you?"

"Well, yeah, that's what I want . . ."

"Is it possible you've been hiding out here?" Jim asked.

"I know I have."

"And how long do you think you can do that?"

Luke's heart lurched. "What do you mean?"

"Don't worry, Luke. It's okay to make a home for yourself here, and you'll always have a job at the hostel . . . We both have an opportunity here. Can you see that?"

"Not really."

"What are you going to do about finishing high school?"

Luke groaned. "How do you know that I haven't?"

"This is me you're talking to. I know more about you than you think. I know more about you than I do about Ava, evidently. Not having a high school diploma will seriously limit your options."

"So at some point I'll do the GED." What was Jim going on about this for? It was so far from Luke's reality. "And I'm not going back to New York."

"I told you, Luke, that I'd be here for you, and I meant it. Will you come back to the hostel now?"

Luke shook his head.

They spent a few moments in silence.

"You're exhausted. C'mon. I'll take you over to Cin's to bunk with her. She'll bring you back in the morning, and we can face this in the light of day."

Luke let himself be led to the car, and once they were at the Airstream he rolled out his sleeping bag beside Cin's trailer as Jim spoke to her. He didn't want to talk anymore and closed his eyes. He heard the trailer door slam and her feet rustle over to him as she stooped down, hands smoothing his forehead.

"The persistence of memory," she whispered, and she placed a small object on his stomach. He waited for the sound of the trailer door again before opening his eyes to see what it was.

Ursula.

three days later and beyond

fifteen

"Have you talked to Luke yet?"

"Not yet. I keep hoping." Everybody, including Ava, had talked to Luke, but not Frank. Ava had brought coffee to Frank and Charlie's cabin, and they sat on the porch, looking out at the La Sal Mountains. Luke had come back after spending the night at Cin's and since then had made himself extremely busy with work or with Tangerine. Frank stayed in the cabin, resting and keeping out of Luke's way. Ava thought it looked like Luke was trying too hard to prove that he had moved on.

Ava had jumped into hostel life, acting *as if.* As if she was comfortable in her own skin, as if she liked people. She had become one of the travelers enchanted by the transformation of the landscape, the transformation of themselves. She could be someone else. Feeling good was definitely discombobulating. She was glad that she had Charlie and Frank to keep her grounded.

"Three more days. Maybe he'll change his mind...but it's enough for me that I'm here, that I'm sober, and that I've been given another chance," Frank said.

• • •

"I think I need to go back home at the end of August," Tangerine said as they watched the movie. Luke hadn't really been concentrating anyway, having seen *Indiana Jones and the Last Crusade* a hundred times already.

"What?" They had been spending every minute they could together for the past few days. "The end of August, that's only two more weeks!" He was on the floor leaning against Tangerine's knees, and she stroked his hair, acting like nothing was changing.

"I miss my family," she said simply. "I'm doomed to be always missing somebody, because when I leave, I'll miss you." She leaned down and kissed his head.

What could he say to that?

"I don't want you to go." There. Tangerine leaned over and put her arms around his chest, squeezing, and he turned her face and kissed her.

"Thank you for saying that," she whispered. "It doesn't change the way I feel about you, you know."

Family. It had been funny watching Jim and Clare with Ava. She was more of a stranger to them than he was. They didn't know how to act around each other. Ava never sat still, while Jim and Clare were much more mellow. She wanted to know everything, while they weren't as intense. Luke never would have become so alienated from his mother. Frank was another story. Luke had successfully avoided him for the past few days. Now Frank, Charlie, and Ava were at an AA meeting. A strange trinity.

The bear flashed before his eyes, and he shuddered. It was persistent, whatever it was.

"Someone walk over your grave?" Tangerine whispered.

"Something like that . . ." He needed to go back to the edge of Moonflower Canyon, up Cable Arch Trail. "Um . . . you wanna go up the cable?"

"Now?"

Something was up there. "Yeah."

"Okay."

He hadn't been out on the mesa in a few days, hadn't used his body, hadn't seen the stars. Maybe he wanted the bear to be real. Maybe he wanted to be a Believer. But he needed at least one witness.

• • •

Ava stood in the parking lot, watching Charlie and Frank head back to their cabin. She had needed that meeting. She was glad that she'd come to Moab, but life was still on life's terms (another winner AA slogan), and there was a serious disconnect between who her parents were at the hostel and who they were to her.

She didn't feel like going to bed and getting lost in her thoughts either. Action was better. So what was she going to do?

She watched Luke and Tangerine come toward her, deep in conversation. Maybe they were going somewhere exciting. But more than likely, they wanted to be alone.

"Hey, guys! What're you doing?" Ava risked asking as they got closer.

"Hey. Uh, we're going up to Cable Arch," Luke said, after a pause.

"Do you want to come?" Tangerine asked.

"Are you sure you don't want to be alone?"

"It's okay. I bet you haven't been up there yet. You should come," Tangerine said.

"Isn't that where—" Ava started to ask.

"Yeah," Luke cut her off. "And anyway, we're taking your dad's car," Luke said. Whatever thoughts had given him pause before were gone now, and Ava's skin prickled with anticipation.

"Hey!" Hal seemed to come out of nowhere. He was a strange dude. "Can I come? Where's Bruno?"

Luke nodded and got in behind the wheel. "Haven't seen him. Must be on a date."

Cable Arch Trail or bust.

• • •

They climbed in silence. Luke was the first up, grasping the cable with a newfound ease.

"Holy shit," Luke heard Ava say. "What is this, Outward Bound? How high is that? I can't see a thing!" Once he was at the top, he pulled out his flashlight and shone it down the face of the sandstone.

"You can do it!" Tangerine encouraged as Ava grabbed the rope and started climbing.

Her face was red from exertion when she got all the way up, but she was laughing at herself. "I did it!" she said as she gave Luke a high five.

Once they were all on the mesa, Luke started walking across, steering away from the precipice. Tangerine kept pace with him, and he reached out for her hand. He wouldn't think about her leaving.

He was trying to keep his head clear, to be in the Zen of hiking, but his thoughts kept centering on Frank and how much he had loved it out here. As far as he knew, Frank kept to the cabin, was too sick to hike.

Some things had appeared outside Luke's trailer. Art supplies, canvases, a mountain bike. Things he had wanted, things he had done without. *What, is he trying to buy me now?*

Charlie would come hang out quite often, chatting with everybody, going for drives, and when Luke asked him about the stuff, he just shrugged. "Maybe you should start painting again, buddy," he said.

Luke's thoughts led him to some of the things he and Frank had learned together, like pitching a tent, rock climbing, swimming even.

Having grown up in New York City, Frank had had to teach himself all of that stuff as an adult, and he wanted Luke to have a basic proficiency. Frank had been willing to try. He had been committed to growth and change—so alive. *How could Mom's death have undone that?* It was very important to Luke to be willing to try. And he felt grateful to Frank for passing that on to him. He realized that was the first time in a long while he had thought about Frank with gratitude.

Maybe he should give his father the benefit of the doubt. But if he really was dying . . . Luke tried to clear his head, counting backward from 100. 100, 99, 98, 97, 96 . . . He began to feel mesmerized by the rocks, putting one foot in front of the other . . . 65, 64, 63, 62 . . . He started to hear drumming. Loud, rhythmic drumming. It sounded like many drummers, but the closer they got, the more clearly they could hear the distinct sound of just one drum. Luke still couldn't see anybody, just hear the sound: *boom, boom, boom.*

Then they saw her, right in front of them. Cin, eyes closed, beating on her drum. She was alone. What should they do? Was this why he'd felt he had to come? Cin had lit three large candles, and as they got closer, Luke could see her face bathed in orange light. Hal and Tangerine sat down and clapped to her beat. Ava held back with him. Luke wanted to run away, but the beat was too hypnotizing. Cin opened her eyes for a second, acknowledging them. It was as if she was expecting them. Luke shrugged. This was better than a bear. He should take a cue from Hal and be able to go with the flow more. No big deal. He sat down and found his hands beginning to keep rhythm.

•   •   •

Heart's full
Moon, stars
Earth
Looklistensmelltastefeelsense

Together
Dance, dance
Life

· · ·

Ava was stunned. The woman began to sing: low and melodic, no words, improvising the sound. They must know this woman, who blended in so much with the landscape that Ava couldn't tell what she looked like. The fire mesmerized Ava, the last one standing. Tangerine stood up again and started moving fluidly in space, creating art with her body. Hal and the woman got up too, clapping, drumming. Ava could see the woman better as she danced by the fire, stripped down to her bathing suit. She was covered in tattoos, and the shadows from the flames made it seem as if the tattoos were dancing too. Animals. A lizard, an elephant? A bear. Ava tried to catch Luke's eyes, but he couldn't take his off Tangerine. And who could blame him? The woman handed the drum to Luke, who was still seated, and he took on the beat. She came toward Ava, beckoning her to dance. *I have to be drunk to do something like this, don't I?* The woman reached out her hand. *What the hell? Act as if.*

· · ·

When Cin gave Luke the drum, he was so surprised that he started drumming and felt his cynicism evaporate. He became willing: this was the willing suspension of disbelief that English teachers were always talking about. It was like going into the world of story, myth.

Luke drummed and watched Cin's sinewy body dance with Tangerine's lushness, Ava's athleticism, and Hal's masculine, aged sorrow. He felt himself stand up and move with them.

He danced with the bear like they were old friends. The moonlight shone down on them like a spotlight, and they moved, entranced. A slight breeze shifted the pattern. The stars twinkled, the rocks vibrated, the air hummed. Luke kept to the beat of the drum as the bear moved through space and time, dancing around them and with them. He felt himself being lifted into her arms, soft fur, voice singing. Then the beat was slowing itself down, his hands tingling, his hips swaying to the ground, sitting. He continued to feel the larger-than-life embrace. Three more beats. Two, one.

The sadness was gone. He hadn't realized how sad he had been. And it was gone. He almost didn't know himself. He was tingling, as if the very particles of his being, atoms and molecules, had shifted to become more than just himself. He felt joined to everyone there and to the earth and the sky. He rubbed his eyes. The bear was gone. Tangerine, Ava, and Hal were staring at him. Luke was staring at Cin.

"Well, that was different," Ava said. "Wow." How long had they been there?

"My favorite time of night," Hal said.

Silence. The five of them sat looking at each other.

What was *that?* they all seemed to think together.

Luke looked up at the sky. The stars had disappeared, and a cloud hovered over them.

"Is it going to rain?" Tangerine wondered. As if on cue, it pelted down on them, water, water in the arid desert.

• • •

It rained and rained and rained. Ava was huddled next to Luke and Tangerine under a thick sandstone arch, trying to stay dry. *Trying* was the operative word. She was soaked! They had all decided not to risk the hike back yet. Flash floods were dangerous, but they didn't last long. It was incredible to watch anyway. Hal had stayed out in the rain.

The sky was getting a little brighter. Was it dawn already? It couldn't be. There was lightning in the distance, followed by a low rumble of thunder.

"Can I get some room service?" Cin yawned. "Cowboy coffee, anyone?" They laughed. Hal had managed to fall asleep, lying on the ground, the rain falling on him.

"Nobody else could sleep through this," Tangerine said.

"Yeah, well, there's nobody like Hal. And nothing like this. How long has this been going on?" Luke checked his watch. "It's three a.m. There's too much lightning to move, but I'm not even tired."

Ava shivered. She still couldn't believe how much of herself she had been able to let go, and how much fun it was. It was probably the most insanely beautiful experience she had ever had. The landscape and the thunderstorm only deepened its power. It was like some kind of science fiction fantasy. She wouldn't have been surprised if a dinosaur had appeared. The whole sky was a blanket of velvety clouds. They watched the lightning rip through the sky and the rain pelt down on the barren earth, making puddles, splashing, changing to darker and darker shades of red, brown, gold.

• • •

Tangerine gave Luke a squeeze. He felt like it was their own private universe, and he felt certain that he loved her, and that he loved Hal too, for that matter, and Cin and Jim and Clare. Ava. The lightning had stopped and it wasn't raining as hard and he saw that Ava had left the group to investigate the rocks farther south.

Cin's back was to him as she pulled her dreadlocks into a ponytail. Her skin was moist with rain, and her tattoos seemed to be vibrating. The bear tattoo.

He couldn't help but reach out a finger and touch the line of the bear's face. "You never told me her name."

"Ursula." Of course. Like his kachina, an obvious enough name for a bear. "You saw her last night, didn't you?" Cin asked, and Luke nodded slowly, wondering if the others were doing the same. He couldn't take his eyes off Cin.

"What are you guys talking about?" Tangerine said.

"You didn't see her?" he asked Tangerine.

"See what?"

Luke gathered his thoughts. "The tattoo."

"Yeah, sure. I've seen it before." She didn't get it, she didn't see. "I need to find the ladies' room," Tangerine said as she stood up and stretched. "Anyone else?"

"Yeah, let's go powder our noses," Ava said, laughing, walking with Tangerine to another boulder in the distance. Luke's eyes followed them for a moment before returning to Cin.

"I definitely saw her," Hal said. "And not for the first time."

"It depends on what you believe, what you see with your heart," Cin said.

"That's right," Hal echoed.

Luke was caught between the mystic and the schizophrenic.

Healer. He could believe that Cin was a healer.

"Is that what you were doing the other night?" Luke asked. "The night we found Jen, I mean." He hesitated. "Were you working with Ursula?"

"Are you suggesting that Ursula brought Jen back to life?" Cin asked.

Luke didn't know what to say. He knew that it sounded ridiculous.

"What do you think? What kind of world do you want to live in? What do you want to believe?"

There was a crash of thunder, and Tangerine rushed back with Ava.

The way the storm broke was astonishing: a deep blue sky had erased the clouds almost like peeling off a sticker, letting them know it was morning. Just as quickly as the storm had come, it passed.

"I guess we should go back down now," Luke said.

"Why? Let's form a utopian society up here and just hang out for the rest of our days," Ava suggested.

"Ava, I do believe that you are one of us, but we are all soaked, and some of us have to get to work." After last night, Cin being the voice of reason was startling, but she was right.

Luke sighed. "We need to be really careful. The rocks are still slick from the rain."

After they shimmied down the cable, they traveled single file.

• • •

It was past 7:00 a.m. when they got back, but Ava still wasn't tired. She felt energized. *God du freaking jour.*

Jim and Clare had been worried about them in the storm, and they were all showered with hugs when they got back. Clare offered to make everyone breakfast. Luke and Jim joined Ava, while Hal disappeared and Tangerine went upstairs to bed. Ava was exhilarated. She was famished, piling eggs on buttered toast.

"What needs doing?" Luke asked Jim.

"Lots of cleaning!"

"Did you go see Jen last night?" Luke asked Clare. "Any word on what happened?"

"How she got to the bottom of a canyon?" Clare answered. "She still won't talk."

"Maybe you should go see her, Luke. Maybe she'd talk to you," Jim said.

"Why would she talk to me?"

"That's a good idea," Clare said. "You're closer to her age, and she doesn't really know you. Sometimes it's easier to talk to people you don't really know . . ."

As great as Ava had been feeling, the rage bubbled up inside her. Why was Jim so focused on Luke? And Clare preoccupied with Jen? What about Ava? Hadn't they been listening to her for the past few days? Why weren't they including her?

"What about me?" She pushed her plate away.

"Yeah, you can go too." Jim looked surprised.

"That's not what I mean. I am right here now, and you still don't see me. I wish that you could have shown as much concern for me the past few years."

"Ava," Jim started. "You were the one who wouldn't communicate, and refused our financial help, and then stopped talking to us altogether. What were we supposed to do?"

"We wanted to give you your space," Clare said. And then, "We wanted to reinvent ourselves."

"But without me?" Ava was close to tears.

"No, honey, never. Never without you," Jim said as he tried to lean closer.

Ava stood up. "But don't you see how it looked to me? Your actions were speaking louder than your words. I come home for a nice weekend with my family before college starts, and you've bought a youth hostel and are packing up my grandmother's house? Don't you understand?"

"Ava! I'm sorry, honey." Clare stood up too.

"What am I doing here?" Ava asked herself.

"Well, I hope you're here to become a family again," Clare said.

Ava shook her head. Was that it? Or was it for the experience she'd had last night? Ava needed a meeting, but there wasn't one until 8:00 that night.

"I have to get out of here for a while. Come on, Luke," Ava said. None of this was his fault. "Let's go see this Jen." At least she could try to help.

● ● ●

Holy shit, Luke thought as Ava stormed out of the hostel. *I would be pissed too.* He got the keys from behind the desk and went to meet her at the car.

"I don't want you to think I'm mad at you," Ava said. "And I know that it's probably too early for visiting hours, but let's go for a drive." Luke handed her the car keys.

Ava smiled weakly. "It just burns me so much that he can be so good at seeing other people—you, for instance—but he looks right through me as if I'm not even there."

"That would bother me too," Luke said. The way it did with Frank.

● ● ●

"I need some serious open road," Ava said.

"Let's go to Dead Horse Point then." They got in the car and Luke directed Ava to drive northwest out of Moab to Route 313, where she would bear south for about twenty miles.

It felt blissful, windows rolled all the way down, being in the only car on the road. She had needed to drive, to feel in control. They sat in silence until they pulled into the turnoff for the point. They both got out of the car, standing at the top and looking down into the wide abyss. The multiple canyons of sandstone were riveting. *Where am I?*

"Why is it called Dead Horse Point?" Ava finally asked.

"One of the stories is that cowboys used to chase wild mustangs up to the point here," Luke said.

Ava closed her eyes for a moment and could almost see the horses. "Good name then," she sighed. "Shadows everywhere."

"It's still one of my favorite places," Luke said. "Name or no name."

Ava felt small, but somehow comforted by the wide expanse.

"You sat with Frank, huh?" Luke asked.

"Yeah, he was in bad shape." Ava looked up at him. "He's not a monster, you know, any more than Jim is."

"I know." Did he really?

"Do you believe that alcoholism is a disease?" Ava asked.

"I know intellectually it is, but it's broken my heart. I can't quite get with that program."

"People can forgive something like cancer much easier, can't they?" Ava mused. "Sometimes though I wish that Jim was an alcoholic, so that I could understand him better. A narcissist is more difficult to forgive."

"Do you really think he's a narcissist? I gotta tell you, I don't see him that way."

"Okay, maybe that is a little harsh, but I'm an extremist. It's all making sense to me now, though. Of course they were too wrapped up in their own problems to see mine, and I completely pushed them away. Maybe *I'm* the narcissist." Luke looked askance at Ava. "Okay again. A couple of freshman psychology classes do not give me the ability to diagnose anybody." She laughed. "But back to Frank. It takes a miracle to get sober."

"There's that word again."

"What, *miracle?* What's wrong with it? I define a miracle only as a shift in perception, not raising the dead, like Tangerine thinks happened to Jen."

"You sound like you're quoting Charlie." Luke scoffed.

"So what? Charlie is one of the only people who make any sense."

155

Luke thought about that. "Well, if that's all a miracle is, then maybe I'll talk to Frank again someday."

"You're making fun of me, but you know that you're gonna have to talk to Frank sooner or later." Ava poked his chest. "In fact, I dare you! I dare you to get over yourself. You keep waiting, it will just get harder. He's only here for a few more days."

She was right. Luke had managed to avoid Frank, and everyone so far was letting him. Not anymore. They got back in the car.

"Is he really dying?" Luke asked softly as Ava started to drive.

She rolled her eyes. "We're all dying. But maybe. I don't mean to be flip, but it doesn't look good. If he can get a new liver, he has a chance."

"Has he even had a biopsy?"

"You're missing the point. He's sober, and he's here *now*. And you'll regret not listening to what he has to say." Luke was quiet. "At least start a conversation," she added.

Luke changed the subject.

"I bet we'll be able to see Jen by the time we get to town."

"Okay, fine." Ava followed Luke's directions to the hospital.

Jen was awake when they got there.

"Hey!" Luke said, going over to stand by her bedside, Ava following.

"Hey," a voice croaked.

"You're still here," Luke said.

"I wish I wasn't," Jen said.

"You mean in the hospital?"

"I wish that I had died," Jen said flatly, and Luke felt cold. He was glad Ava was there. "Who are you?" Jen asked Ava.

"I'm Clare and Jim's daughter—from the Moonflower?"

"Oh. They're great."

"Yeah, I hear that all the time. My name's Ava. So. What's your story?"

Luke raised his eyebrows at Ava. *Easy.*

Jen looked at the space between them. "Why should I tell you? I haven't told anybody anything. It's not going to help. Nothing feels good anymore."

"I don't think that you could shock me," Ava said. "I've done some pretty crazy things too."

"Really?" Jen asked, and their eyes connected.

"Really. Dangerous things." Ava paused. "And then humiliating things. Before I knew it, I wanted to end my life, the pain was so bad."

"Me too," Jen whispered. "I wanted to die."

"I had no hope anymore," Ava said. She reminded Luke of Frank.

"I should be dead." Jen's face was all scrunched up, like she was going to cry. She took a deep breath instead. "I met this guy Jaime earlier this summer, and we fell in love. I thought." She paused. "I don't want to talk about this."

"You don't have to," Ava said. "Right, Luke?"

They were all quiet for a few moments.

Luke looked out the window and said, "Do you want us to leave?" He felt Jen's eyes on him and turned toward her. Jen had tears streaming down her face; she was shaking her head. "It's okay, we'll stay," he said, and sat down in one of the chairs. Ava did the same.

"Okay. I started tweaking on crystal meth with him, because I wanted him to like me, but then I wanted to do it because I loved the way it made me feel. Fast-forward. We had been doing crystal for two days with some of his friends. We thought it would be fun to be high on the cliffs, somewhere where there weren't many tourists.

"Jaime hooked up with this other girl," Jen sobbed.

Luke looked down. Ava pulled her chair closer to Jen, giving her time to cry, then reaching to hand her a tissue from her bedside table.

"Ouch. I've been there," Ava said. "And then I bet you stopped feeling good from the crystal?"

Jen nodded, blowing her nose. "It gets worse. I flipped out. He was making out with her, right in front of me, you know? He called me a freak, and he and his friends left me there, laughing."

"And I bet all you wanted was to do more crystal?"

"Yes. I can't believe you know how I feel," Jen said between sobs. "But there was nothing left, so I jumped."

"You jumped?" Luke said.

"I told you. I wanted to die. And then I hallucinated a bear."

• • •

"Wow," Luke said as they left the hospital.

Ava felt shaken. "*Wow* is right. Don't you want to find that kid Jaime and hang him by his toes?"

"I bet he's long gone by now," he said. "But you and Frank really are wired the same way."

Then Ava badgered Luke about talking to Frank the whole drive back to the hostel, only stopping to listen for Luke's monotone directions. Who wasn't a little rough around the edges?

• • •

Luke found himself in front of Frank's cabin. Frank and Charlie were sitting on the porch, reading aloud from Shakespeare's *Twelfth Night*. He almost laughed. They were such geeks, but at least it was a comedy. They'd had enough tragedy. And Frank wasn't in bed moping like he used to. Charlie spotted Luke, said something about a cup of coffee, and walked over to the main building. Luke leaned against the porch railing. He wasn't going to sit, he wasn't going to say anything. What could he say?

Frank put down the book. He took a deep breath. "Saying sorry just doesn't cut it, what I've done to you. And I'm not asking for your forgiveness. I just don't want you to carry around anger toward a deadbeat, drunk dad for the rest of your life. I want to take responsibility for my behavior, and its impact on you. I'm not going to hide behind my disease anymore."

Luke looked at the mountains in the east, his mind racing.

"I'm proud of you, Luke. When I finally stopped drinking, when I came to, I could barely sleep because of the nightmares I was having about you. I had to come out and make sure that you were all right. And you are, you are." Frank paused, the silence stretching. Was Luke supposed to say something? Thank you? "I'm going back to New York to get my life together. I need to act as if I'm going to live, to heal. Maybe at some point you'll want to come back . . . Is there any way I can make it up to you?"

Luke shook his head. It was all too much. Then he actually said something. "No. I'm going to stay here for now."

"Maybe when we've figured some stuff out on our own, we can talk again?"

Luke nodded. This was all he could handle for now. "Yeah." He looked up, straight into Frank's eyes, clear and untroubled, and he knew that Frank loved him.

• • •

The week had passed, and it was Tuesday afternoon again. Frank and Charlie were leaving. Ava and Luke stood at the bottom of the driveway, waving to the back of the rental car.

"They're coming back for Christmas," Luke said, "if Frank makes it."

"He'd better make it, or I'll kick his ass. Charlie will take care of him. Hell, I'll take care of him when I get to New York in a couple of weeks."

"Are you glad you changed your ticket?"

Ava didn't know how to answer Luke's question. *Glad* wasn't exactly the right word. Clare and Jim seemed frantic, trying to make up for everything right away, overwhelming her. She was trying to be honest about her feelings, but it was hard work.

"Maybe it's just the next right thing. I'll go back before school starts. Clare's coming with me."

"Good," Luke said firmly, and she felt a rush of affection for him. He wasn't completely blinded by his love for Jim and Clare.

"You're doing the right thing too," she said softly, catching his eye.

"And what would that be?"

"You patched things up with Frank but you're not rushing it. I find that pretty impressive. And I'm a little jealous!"

"Really?"

"Really. It's all a little too close for comfort for me sometimes, but, I don't know. I guess I wouldn't have it any other way."

"Yeah. I've noticed that Jim's been hovering over you lately, since you told him off."

"Funny thing is, I've always wanted Jim to hover, but now that he is, I don't know how to handle it. At least there are AA meetings in town every night, and I have you to talk to." Jim had also offered to pay her living expenses in New York so that she could focus on her studies and sobriety. She had accepted immediately, agreeing that she had been both stubborn and foolish.

"Families are so complicated," Ava said with a sigh. "It must be hard for you, seeing Frank weak and sick."

"True. I don't want to watch him die, but I've seen him worse, believe me. What are we doing outside in this heat?"

"Changing the subject, huh?" Ava nudged him. "Okay. Are you going to the hospital now or later?" For the past week they had made sure to visit Jen often.

"Might as well go soon. I want to stop by Red Rock and see Tangerine too."

Ava nodded. "Is she really leaving?"

"I've convinced her to stay until just before Labor Day. Cin needs her."

Ava smiled. "Cin needs her, huh?"

Luke ignored the jibe. "She misses her family. All of these reunions have her feeling a bit misty. She says she's coming back."

"But you're sad."

"Yeah, I guess I am—about that. But in another sense I feel like my whole life has opened up. I live in a world now where I don't have to hide. And I have to trust that if it's meant to be, it will be."

"That sounds a little abstract for you! Charlie says, *More will be revealed . . . let go and let God . . .* "

Luke shrugged. "Don't go crazy now. There's also *live and let live.* So what else can I do?"

"Okay," Ava said. She couldn't stand out in the sun any longer. "Twenty minutes? I bet you want to see if Tangerine can take the rest of the day off. Let's go in Clare's car. The air conditioner works so much better!"

• • •

Luke surveyed the painting, *his* painting. Yesterday he had been drawn to a canvas, to blues and grays with a tinge of purple. It had turned into a portrait of Frank, mournful, regretful, hopeful. Something still wasn't right. Luke didn't want Frank's disease to define him anymore. Saying goodbye had helped. And he had to admit, so had saying hello. He quickly found his brushes, the red and orange paints, superimposing the mask of a bear over his father's face: Frank dressed as a kachina. He stood back, looking at the painting. There was Ursula again. Could it be heat-induced psychosis? He laughed at himself. Maybe he didn't need to be so scared of mystery, of letting go, of imagination, of life.

He walked out of his trailer into the blazing sun, hoping that Ava had already revved up the AC in the Camry. He saw her blond head bobbing up and down in the driver's seat, and he smiled.

"So you're driving?" he said, easing into the passenger seat. The air felt good.

"You'd better get used to it, buddy." It felt good to have friends.

acknowledgments

I should probably thank everybody in my life for putting up with me over all the years that *Edges* has been in my head, but I will try to be brief and acknowledge only those who supported me in getting my ideas down on paper and *Edges* into book form.

I owe a huge debt of gratitude first to my mother, Josephine, who read the first pages I wrote and continues to be a source of encouragement and support; to my friend and mentor Sandra Jordan, who read my first draft (which had nine different points of view and was a *Tales of the City* meets *Dawson's Creek* kind of thing) and gently suggested I stick to the teen POV; to my husband, Rob, whom I met at a youth hostel in Moab, Utah (strangely enough), and who is a fierce editor; to my sister, Charlotte, who read drafts and acted as both spokesperson and cheerleader when it came to getting an agent; to Edward Necarsulmer, my agent, who understood and believed in the book and was a rigorous taskmaster in setting the standards high, working with me through two more drafts before sending the manuscript to Farrar Straus Giroux.

My heart fills to the brim with appreciation for Margaret Ferguson, my amazing editor, who took a chance on this first-time author and who helped me find the right tone for *Edges*. I am also grateful to her brilliant assistant, Beth Potter, whose guidance through this process has been invaluable; for the copy editors, Karla Reganold and Susan Brown, and their understanding of nuance; for the jacket designer, Natalie Zanecchia, and all the others at Farrar Straus Giroux who make publishing a book like this possible.

And, finally, these acknowledgments would never be complete without an honorable mention to my late grandmother, Madeleine L'Engle, whose spirit has been with me throughout, and who taught me invaluable lessons about faith and art.